MURDER
ME TENDER

MAX GRIFFIN

MURDER ME TENDER
Copyright © 2013 MAX GRIFFIN
ISBN 978-1-61292-091-7
ISBN 10: 1612920918

Cover Art Designed by Anastasia Rabiyah
Photographs Copyright Dreamstime.com
Edited by Shoshana Hurwitz and Traci Markou

Published by Purple Sword Publications, LLC
Tucson, Arizona, USA
www.PurpleSword.com

Chapter One

"Take My Breath Away"
July 2008

Rick tipped his head and squinted at the squiggly checkers of orange and red that littered the canvas. "What do you think of this one, Sandra? It's only twenty-five thousand. A steal at that price."

She sniffed and muttered in his ear, "More like grand theft, if you ask me. It's fine, if you're looking for linoleum patterns for McDonald's restrooms." She squeezed his arm. "I need a drink if I'm going to have to look at much more of this crap. Be a dear, will you, and bring me some white wine?"

He pulled his arm free and inched away from his sister-in-law. "Sure. I saw a guy around here someplace." He surveyed the gallery and spotted the cute Latino server he'd noticed earlier.

His gaze lingered on the young man's tight backside, and a faint thrill pulsed in his loins before he tore his eyes away. He glanced at the safer visage of his companion and muttered, "I'll be right back."

She clutched at his arm and pulled herself close again. "I'll go with you." She peered at the painting. "You know, I could swear I've seen this hideous thing someplace else. Your office, maybe?"

He let his face relax into a smile while he grabbed two glasses from the serving tray.

"Actually, there's one by the same artist hanging in the bank's boardroom. It's been there forever, even before your father hired me. That's why I had the bank co-sponsor this show."

"Victoria decorated that room for Daddy. This looks like something good ol' Sis would pick out. She's the artsy one, and this is the kind of thing she'd go ga-ga over."

His face froze at the mention of his wife's name. "It's a shame she's not here tonight. She so enjoys gallery openings."

Sandra leaned into him and whispered, "I'm sorry. I know her disappearance is a painful topic for you. But if she were here, she'd just be making your life miserable with some nasty complaint. I don't understand why you're still pining for her after the way she's treated you." Her hands plucked at her lace shawl and rearranged it about her bare shoulders.

Rick sighed. "I keep thinking that one of these days she'll just reappear, like nothing happened."

She snorted. "Yeah, like she's going to show up from wherever she's run off to with the trust fund money. She's gone for good, or more likely for bad." She stopped, and her gaze raked over him. "Frederick Collier, I just don't know what I'm going to do with you. You're still trim and athletic, and you were always good looking." Her fingers laced through his hair, and her voice mellowed. "You're turning a little gray, but my hairdresser could make those curls the same chestnut-brown you had in college. You don't have to be alone, you know. You'd be quite a catch."

He brushed her hand aside. "Stop, please. And we should at least give Victoria the benefit of the doubt; after all, she's your sister, besides being my wife. We don't know she actually stole that money. She only took what she's legally entitled to." He sighed. "She and I are still husband and wife, despite everything. Can't we agree to disagree on this, at least for tonight?"

"I guess." She hooked arms with him and they strolled through the crowded gallery, pushing their way past the tuxedos and dazzling evening gowns of Chicago's elite.

He nodded to a passing bank customer and decided to change the subject. "I appreciate you coming with me tonight," he whispered. "It looks better for the business at social events like this if I have someone on my arm. Especially so, since you're also on the bank's board."

Her lips turned down, and she frowned. She started to speak, but paused as if to compose herself. The rubies on her fingers glittered as she toyed with her pearl necklace. After a moment, she stopped before another painting. "I enjoyed coming, even to see this grotesque excuse for art. It gave me a reason to get into the city." She beamed at him. "Tell you what. For payback, you can take me shopping tomorrow. Now that I've wasted my dress for this shindig, I'll need a new one for the opera next month. Can't wear the same thing twice in public, you know."

Visions of endless hours wasted in exclusive shops on Michigan Avenue flashed through his mind. He tried to control his expression. "Well, you know I am grateful and all, but I've got some things at the bank I have to attend to tomorrow. After all, the business pays the bills for all of us."

She dimpled and poked him in the shoulder. "You're so cute when you think you're trapped. Silly, I'm not like your wife. Victoria liked making you do things she knew you hated."

She tipped her head, and her smile turned coy. "Maybe we could have lunch tomorrow, though? Someplace quiet?"

"Quiet? In the Loop? Surely you jest."

She chortled and tossed her head. Her auburn hair caught the bright lights and glowed like a tarnished halo over her midnight black gown. "How about Ajasteak? It's only a few blocks from the bank. We used to go there, once upon a time."

He stopped and inspected her features, remembering. "Are you sure? We haven't been there in ages. Not since...."

She held a finger to his lips. "Don't say it. It's fine. You can have steak, and I'll have sushi. It'll be like old times, except now we're relatives, thanks to good ol' Sis." She tugged at his arm. "Come on. Let's check out the next room. Maybe this person learned how to paint!"

As they turned the corner, she smiled at a passing acquaintance. "So nice to see you, Dr. Warren." She reached out and clasped the older man's hand. "I'm Sandra Montgomery. We met at the Opera Board Charity Ball."

The elderly, overweight gentleman nodded at her.

Rick stared at the muscle boy, who followed a step behind the man. The young man's tuxedo rippled against his body and accented his broad shoulders and narrow hips. *He looks like a wide receiver trapped by some twist of fate in a Fitzgerald novel.* The young man locked eyes with him, and Rick jerked his attention to Warren's pudgy features.

He dug into his memory, came up with the old man's first name, and his balance with the bank. *Better be careful. He's pretty temperamental, and the firm can ill afford to lose an account of that size.* He plastered a smile on his features and extended his hand. "Peter, always good to see you. Rick Collier here." Their hands touched; Warren's was slimy with perspiration.

"Yes, of course, Frederick Collier, from Montgomery Savings and Trust. You had a party at that estate of yours, the one way out in the country. What's the name of the place again?"

"You mean our home in Wisconsin. Lindermont Manor. Perhaps you can come visit us again? The bank is planning another fete for our best customers next spring."

"Perhaps we shall, indeed. And how is your delightful wife?" He fanned his face with the gallery program. "I forget her name. Is she here?"

Rick's lips turned cold and he stammered, but Sandra rescued him. "That would be my sister, Victoria, Dr. Warren. She was weary of high society and went to Europe last spring to pursue her interest in painting." Rick gaped at her, and then closed his mouth.

"Ah. I'm so glad the rumors were untrue. Perhaps one day we'll attend *her* opening."

Warren's eyes roamed the room, and he started to move on.

The muscle boy cleared his throat and tugged at his master's sleeve.

A frown tried to wrinkle Warren's Botox-smoothed brow. "Oh, where are my manners?" His indifferent tone failed to hide his annoyance. "Let me introduce you to my companion. Brandon, this is Mr. Frederick Collier. He manages some of my accounts over at Montgomery Savings and Trust. And this is his sister-in-law, Ms. Sandra Montgomery."

"Brandon, so nice to meet you." Rick gripped a calloused hand and gazed into blue eyes as deep as the ocean.

"Ms. Montgomery. Mr. Collier. It is my distinct pleasure to make your acquaintance."

Brandon gave a little bow while his bold gaze stayed locked on Rick's brown orbs.

The youth's quiet tenor danced a slow tango with Rick's heart. He caught his breath and looked away—at Sandra's coiffure, at Warren's bald pate, at the hideous paintings, at anything but the alluring masculine form in front of him.

Warren huffed and scowled. "Well, then, that's done. I see the artist, and I simply must tell her how much I admire her magnificent work." Warren nodded at Sandra and Rick. "Come along, Brandon." The two wandered off into the crowd, with Rick's eyes tarrying on the muscle boy's backside.

Sandra followed his gaze, and a small smile played over her lips. She breathed a quiet sigh and leaned into him. "We were discussing your missing wife."

He startled, turned back to face her, and scowled. "What were you thinking, telling him that Victoria was studying painting in Europe?"

"It's none of his business where she's at. You want I should tell him she ripped off the Trust my parents left us and abandoned you?"

"Well, it's the truth."

"He's creepy. I didn't feel like telling him what that witch did to you. Some nasty comment would just ooze out of his mouth and plop onto the floor, stinking the place up." She beamed at him. "You know, now that I think of it, he reminds me of Victoria."

He cast a furtive glance to be sure Warren was gone and leaned in to whisper to her. "Shush, now. I wish you wouldn't talk that way about your sister. I know you and Victoria haven't gotten along since...well, you haven't always gotten along. A lot of that's my fault. But she's your only sister, so I wish you'd give her a break." He took her arm and pretended to stroll and look at the paintings. "I know you're right; Victoria can be mean. But she can be wonderful, too. It's not all bad with her." He fought a losing battle to keep his manner steady.

"Sure. That's why she vanished without so much as a fare-thee-well, leaving you in the lurch. To say nothing of taking millions out of our inheritance. You have a right to part of that money, you know, so she screwed you, too. Still, as far as I'm concerned, it's just as well that she's gone. Freddy, she's not coming back. You need to get on with your life."

"Rick. Please call me Rick. Victoria's the only one who calls me Freddy." He couldn't look her in the eye.

"I know. Except I called you Freddy too, back when you and I were dating. I think she calls you that now just to annoy me. And to annoy you, too, I suppose." She pulled away from him, and a sigh gusted from her depths. "Rick. You should really divorce her, you know? Face it, she's gone for good."

He frowned and looked around at the other patrons. "This isn't the place, Sandra."

"Well, what is the place? Are you worried about the Montgomery Investment Trust or the business? Is it the scandal? I know that's all the idiots on the Board care about. God knows the missing money and her...other activities make it clear what she did. But between the disappearance and her affairs, you've got more than enough to break the prenup and divorce her. I'd testify, if you needed it, at the proceedings. Close the books and move on."

Heat flushed his face. "Sandra, please! Can we not discuss this?" He stared into her eyes and looked away. The glimmering evening attire of the crowd danced about them. "This is a private showing, and some of the bank's biggest customers are here."

"The bank! You know, Rick, you've buried yourself in that damned bank since this all happened. It's not good for you. You should take a vacation. Maybe we could go together. Fly off to Rio. Or Greece."

"I could use a vacation," he mused. He flashed her a smile. "Wouldn't that look good? The chairman of the board runs off with his sister-in-law to Rio after his wife has gone to

God knows where. You heard Peter. There's already gossip." He paused. "You know, your story about her being in Europe to study art isn't all that bad. It's a credible cover to tell people like Warren when they ask."

She shook her head, and golden highlights shimmered in her hair. "You don't need to tell people like him anything. You always care what these phonies think. Well, I don't care one whit!" She peered into his eyes, and her expression softened. "She's gone. You don't need to hide anymore, you know?"

He reached out to touch her cheek with a bent forefinger, but she jerked back. "Sandra, you know that there can't be anything between us, not anymore. Please don't make a scene. That's not like you." He caught the glisten of unshed tears as her eyes fluttered.

"That's not what I meant! I know it's over between us. I was thinking of you, that you shouldn't be alone. You don't have to hide, you know." She wiped at her eyes, and her mascara smeared. "Good old Sandra. She never makes a scene, no matter what." She snorted. "I'm the loyal sister who only thinks of others. Well, now I'm thinking of you." She grabbed his hand and held it to her face. "I still love you, you know? I never stopped loving you. It hurts so much to see you alone and unhappy." Her voice was a low undertow to the flood of conversation about them.

"Dear Sandra. I love you. You know that. It's just not the same with us." He squeezed her hand. "You have forgiven me so much. Can you forgive me my dream that things will return to normal?"

She sniffed and swiped at her nose. "I'm sorry. I guess I'm being cruel, pushing you like this." She gazed around the room. "I must look a fright. I bet my mascara has run and I'm doing a raccoon imitation. Let me toddle off to the ladies' room for a moment, will you? I'll fix myself all up, then we can go to dinner. I promise I'll be better." She pulled her shawl about her shoulders, raised her head high, and strode through the crowded room.

Rick snagged a fresh glass of Chablis from one of the waiters and rambled about. Careful to have his wandering appear random, he placed himself near Warren and his male companion.

The older man engaged the artist in animated conversation while his escort stood nearby with a smile on his face and a glint in his eye. Rick's hungry gaze looked away from the broad shoulders and the chiseled features. *The old troll brought a paid escort, and a male one at that. He's got balls, I'll give him that.* He sipped his wine and eavesdropped.

The artist blathered, her voice as artless as her paintings. "My studio is in Sedona, you know. It's a wonderful place for creative people." Her long, red hair hung like a cape down her back, almost as though she'd ironed it to make it extra straight. A tattoo of a snake slithered around her shoulder and disappeared underneath her meager bodice.

Warren's voice gurgled up from his throat. "What a coincidence! We're headed out to Sedona ourselves next week." He draped a pudgy arm over Brandon's shoulder. "Madonna is letting us use her place while she's in Italy shooting a movie." He paused and blew his nose on his cocktail napkin. "You know, there's all kinds of spiritual vortexes out there in Sedona."

"Vortices." Brandon's quiet tones teased the soul, even when they were but a whisper.

Rick inhaled the heady musk scent that wafted his way. He ignored Warren's bulging eyes and florid face and edged closer to the vision of masculine perfection that made this night worthwhile.

The old man growled at his companion. "What did you say?"

"I think the plural of 'vortex' is 'vortices.' That's all."

"Well, aren't you the smart one? Where did you get *your* doctorate again?"

Brandon paled. "I don't have one. You know that, Peter."

"Exactly. So don't correct your betters." He turned back to the snake-woman. "Now, where were we? Oh yes. Perhaps the three of us can have dinner next week when we're in Sedona? Do you have a card? I'll give you a call."

Rick relaxed as Sandra's arm slipped around his waist and she whispered in his ear. "There you are. Can we leave this awful place?"

"Sure. I'll call us a cab."

"Fine, but let's wait in the lobby, okay? I've got to get away from all these phonies."

He cast one last look at Brandon before he led the way to the exit. While they waited for their cab, he held her hand and smiled. "You know, I've been thinking you're right. Maybe we should take a vacation. Have you ever been to Sedona?"

Chapter Two

"Don't Know Much About Algebra"

Brandon squirmed in his chair and peered at the text on his laptop screen. He pulled out a yellow notepad and copied down Greek letters and mathematical symbols from the computer. His eyes focused on his notes, brow furrowed, while his pencil tapped on the desktop.

Peter muted the television, where a bearded guy with an annoying voice was hawking some mail-order product. "Brandon, you look so cute sitting there in your underwear. What are you doing?"

"My calculus homework," he muttered, still staring at his computer screen.

"But we're supposed to be on vacation. Can't you do that later?"

Brandon wondered for a moment what it would be like if there was a mute button for Peter. He sighed and turned to the older man. "I'm sorry, Peter. I'd rather be doing things with you, but I'm already behind in this course."

Peter nodded his head, and his double chins wagged. "Didn't you have a nice time today?"

"Yeah. Sedona is beautiful. Thank you for bringing me here. When I was a kid on the south side, we were just poor, white trash. I never imagined then that I'd ever come to a place like this, let alone stay in Madonna's home."

"Well then, enjoy it while you can. Stop being such a bore about your homework." He patted the bed next to him. "Be a dear and come rub my feet. They're so tired after all the walking we did today." The stream of commercials ended, and Peter unmuted the sound.

Brandon glanced at the television. *Right. Keanu Reeves as a self-educated nuclear physicist. Now that's believable. About as believable as me getting a degree.* He shook his head. "I'll just be another thirty minutes or so. If I can't figure out how they integrated this by then, I'll never do it."

"Come on, calculus can wait." He wiggled his pudgy toes. "What does it matter if your homework is late?"

"If I miss another assignment, I'll have to drop the course and start over again. Just another thirty minutes. Maybe less, if I can figure it out."

"So drop the course already. I'm paying the tuition, after all. What difference does it make?"

"It means I have to start all over again, and I'm that much further from finishing my degree. I know you want me to graduate." He hid his disappointment by flipping through his textbook.

"Yes, of course, but there's no reason to be in such a rush. I'll take care of you, now and forever." He patted the bed again. "Come here, I need you," he wheedled.

Brandon sighed. "All right, but then can I finish my assignment later? When you're asleep?"

"Now, you know that computer screen and the clack of the keyboard keeps me awake. Really, don't be such a buzzkill."

Brandon shuddered at Peter's attempt to be hip. "I'll take my laptop in the other room. This place is huge. I won't bother you. You'll let me work later, okay? Promise me?"

"Whatever." Peter loosened the tie on his sweatpants, and the head of his erect cock popped free. "Come on, I need you."

Brandon gave his homework one last, lingering glance and pushed away from the desk. He stood and stretched.

"That's my boy!" Peter slipped his baggy sweatpants over his hips and exposed his paunch and his hard cock. "Show me that beautiful body, boy."

Brandon forced a smile to his lips. He slipped his fingers under his jockey shorts and wiggled his hips. "Is there some part of my body you'd like to see?"

"You know the parts I like best. Do it now." Peter's voice snapped with command while he wallowed in the bed, stripping from the waist down. His T-shirt, stained with coffee and doughnut crumbs, twisted up his torso and exposed his flabby belly.

Brandon slipped out of his shorts and posed for his master. His flaccid cock flopped between his legs like an enormous hose. His hands crept up the treasure trail of hair from his crotch to the auburn thatch that covered his chest. He lingered for a moment on his nipples before his fingers toyed with the chain and padlock that hung about his neck. "What would you like me to do, Peter?"

"You should make that thing hard for me first." Peter's hand pumped at his cock while his gaze locked on Brandon's crotch. "Go ahead, play with it."

A trickle of excitement flashed from his inner roots and out his balls. Brandon's left hand played with his nipples while his right hand stroked his cock. He stared into his master's eyes and the other's lust resonated with his soul, filling a need deep within his being. His cock responded by swelling in his hand into a steel rod of pleasure. His own profound need to give of himself to another danced in perfect harmony with Peter's lascivious demands.

"That's it, boy. Jack that thing." Peter leaned over and pulled lube and a condom from his nightstand. "Come here, boy. I've got something for you." He waved his cock while he applied the clear gel to its head and slipped on the latex.

He straddled the old man, and his face relaxed into an honest grin. "Give it to me, sir. I need you inside me." Peter's fingers, slick with K-Y, massaged his cock and he gasped in pleasure. "Oh fuck, that's nice."

"You like that, do you, boy? Does it feel good?" Peter's husky voice rasped in his ears, but his fingers were smooth as silk. They roamed lower to tug at Brandon's balls, then further back, to tease him. "Tell me what you need, boy."

It was in these moments, when his master was focused on him and nothing but him, that Brandon knew he was alive. He panted and rolled his hips, his hard cock flexing and fucking air. "I need you inside me, sir. Do it to me. Please!"

"That's it, boy. That's what you want."

Two fingers, three, then more entered Brandon's hole. He relaxed his sphincters and shuddered in the pleasure of surrender while he basked in Peter's rapt gaze. "More, sir, more!"

Peter played with him, entering and withdrawing his fist and indulging their mutual need. "Time for me to fuck you, boy." He guided his cock backward, slipped it behind Brandon's balls, and used his hand to find the sweet spot. His eyes closed and his breaths came in rhythms, ancient and profane. He moaned as his hips thrust down into the bed, then up into Brandon, rocking back and forth. On the television, Keanu peered at a cold fusion reactor boiling with energy.

Peter's entry into his body exalted Brandon and uplifted him to heaven. His hands drifted backward and locked behind his head while his hips rotated. His body, his very being, pivoted on the nexus that was Peter's hard desire. "Oh God, yes. Fuck me. Split me in half. Do it to me!" His words came in whispered gasps, evidence of a consciousness that vibrated between the pleasure of submission and the agony of unrequited lust.

Peter's body spasmed, and he cried out. His fingers tore into Brandon's buttocks, and the muscles in his face writhed in a paroxysm of prurient hunger that he sated by consuming Brandon's body. His hips rose, his fists clenched, and his eyes clamped shut as his fluids jetted out, and Brandon imagined them filling his body. The moment stretched to infinity, but then slithered to an indelicate halt.

"That was good, boy." Peter pushed him away and glanced at the spent rubber that despoiled the sheets. "Get me a towel, will you?"

A huge sigh escaped from Brandon's depths as he slipped off his master and knelt by his side. He gloried at the sight of the cum still leaking from Peter's cock. A warm trickle of lube ran down the inside of his left thigh, and his ass burned from his surrender. He knew he was complete. "God, you do that so good, Peter. Better than anyone."

The old man reached out and ran his fingers over Brandon's still hard cock. They circled the head and swiped at the precum leaking from its tip. "You're so beautiful. Do you want to jack off to finish?"

""No. I like being like this, not cumming. That way I know it's all about you, about giving to you." He bounced off the bed. "Let me get you your towel."

"Don't forget to rub my feet."

* * * *

The next morning, Brandon awoke before dawn. He peered at the digital clock. *Nearly six a.m. Plenty of time to finish my homework before the tour today.* He looked around for his underwear, but couldn't find it. Peter snorted and stirred on the bed. *Don't want to wake him up.* He shrugged, gathered his laptop and notes together, and padded, still naked, to the kitchen.

Before long, the scent of coffee filled the room and the sun peeked over the towering red bluffs and slanted through the windows. This morning, the integrals that had so puzzled him the night before flowed with no effort onto the page. The elegant simplicity of the equations, the way they fit together in divine perfection, filled him with a sense of unity with the universe. It was almost as beautiful as the way their two bodies fit together the night before. By eight, he completed his homework and closed his laptop. He ambled onto the deck, gazed at the peaks high over the valley, and let the sun warm his body.

"Brandon! What are you doing, naked outdoors, like an animal?" Peter stared at him from the kitchen, a cup of coffee in his hands and wisps of hair floating over his bald head. He still wore the stained T-shirt and sweatpants from last night.

"There's no neighbors who can see. The nearest house with a view of the deck is way on the other side of the valley."

"Yes, and Madonna told me that the paparazzi hang out over there with telephoto lenses. You get back in here."

"So what if they take a picture of me?" He turned and flopped his genitals at the distant hills. "I'm nobody. If they publish pictures of me, then maybe I'll be somebody. Give me and them a thrill."

"Don't be silly. *I'm* not nobody, and neither is our hostess. Put some underwear on and fix me breakfast."

Before long, the odors of bacon frying and omelets sizzling filled the room. Brandon stood at the stove and beamed. "I'm looking forward to our tour today, aren't you?"

"Hmm? What tour is that?" Peter didn't look up from the newspaper.

"I signed us up yesterday. It's a tour of the valley by a Native American guide. He'll tell us their legends and take us to those vortices you mentioned."

"Oh yes, I do recall, now that you mention it. That sounds perfectly boring. You run along without me."

Disappointment flared in him, and he turned back to the griddle. "I'd like us to go together. It's nice when we share things."

"We shared things last night." He turned the page on the paper and folded it in half.

"I meant something besides sex. Here's your omelet. You want orange juice?"

"I'll have tomato juice, thank you."

Brandon served them juice and coffee and sat at the table. "So how about it? Can we go together?"

"No, I've got some reading to do today. You run along." He glanced at the empty table in front of his companion. "Aren't you going to have breakfast?"

"After I work out." He sighed. "The tour leaves at eleven. You sure you won't go?"

"I said no. But you know what? You wanted to drive that sports car we rented yesterday. Now's your chance. You'll have to take it to wherever this thing starts. Doesn't that sound like fun?" He didn't look up from the financial section.

Brandon sighed. "Sure. Thanks."

"Just be careful. I don't want to have to pay for speeding tickets or for an accident."

"I'll be careful. I always am." He waited, but Peter said nothing more. "I think I'll go work out now. I'll clean up later, if that's all right."

"Whatever." Peter turned the paper over and sipped his coffee.

The agency was crammed into a strip mall next to the tourist hotels. The sign in the window said *Sedona Jeep Tours, Best in Arizona*. Brandon entered and rang the bell on the counter. An older woman, lean and gray, appeared from the back. She wore a skirt and blouse that would have looked at home on Annie Oakley, and a large turquoise and silver pendant hung from a leather strap about her neck. Her leathery face broke into a smile when she saw him.

"What can I do for you, son?"

"I've got reservations for the eleven o'clock tour. Warren, party of two. Except that Mr. Warren won't be here, so it'll just be me."

She checked her log book. "Sure 'nuff. There's another couple what's on your tour, but they's not here yet. Eddie'll be your guide. He's out washin' his jeep off. There's coffee if you want. Otherwise, jest take yourself a sit over there, and you'll be off in no time." She nodded to a wood bench next to the doorway.

Brandon picked up a pamphlet with the itinerary for today's outing and browsed through it while he waited. He glanced up when the door chimed open. A handsome man, his chestnut hair flecked with gray, entered and strode to the counter. Recognition flashed through him, and he controlled the twitch in his loins. *It's that guy from the art gallery last week. God, he's beautiful.* He looked back at the pamphlet. *Totally out of my class, that's for sure. Straight, too. Just my luck.* Visions of last night with Peter echoed in his head, and a vague longing for something more made his soul mourn.

"Collier, party of two for the eleven o'clock tour. Except my sister-in-law has a headache and won't be joining us, so it's just me."

Brandon's chest thudded at the timbre of that voice, and he controlled his breathing. The guy's baritone, so confident and sure, plucked at his heartstrings and made them sing. *God, why are all the perfect guys straight?*

"Yes, sir. Your guide Eddie's just cleanin' up his jeep. The tour'll start in no time. There's coffee if you want." She nodded to the pot of blackened liquid that fumed in one corner of the counter.

His eyes twinkled. "I think I'll pass, thanks."

"Well, then, jest have yourself a sit." She returned to her desk.

He turned, glanced at Brandon, and his face paled. He looked away and meandered over to the stand with the brochures.

Brandon frowned. *He didn't seem stuck-up at the gallery. Maybe he just can't remember my name and he's embarrassed. No reason I can't at least be friendly.* He stood and cleared his throat. "Mr. Collier? I think we met last week in Chicago. Peter Warren is a mutual friend. I'm Brandon." The other turned, and a smile lit his face. Brandon's breath quickened.

"Yes, I recall." He extended his hand. "It's so nice to see you. Will Peter be joining us today?"

For an instant, Brandon lost himself in the depths of those brown eyes. The other's hand warmed him, and an electric thrill pulsed from that grip through his marrow and into his soul. He couldn't look away, couldn't let go. "Uh, no. Peter had business to do. So it's just me."

"Well, my sister-in-law decided not to come either. So I guess it's just the two of us. How nice. Perhaps we can get to know one another better." Their hands remained joined as if neither could stand the thought of separation.

The door chimed open again, and a muscular young man with skin of bronze and a ponytail hanging to his hips entered. His face creased in a broad smile, and he put his hand over Brandon's and Rick's. "You must be my guests today. Welcome."

Annie Oakley looked up from her paperwork. "You're late, Eddie. What time will you have them back?"

"We might be a bit later than usual, but we'll be back not much after sunset." His gaze raked over the other two men. "I've had a vision that the Great Spirit has something special in mind for us today."

Chapter Three

"Good Vibrations"

Rick settled into the backseat of the battered jeep and let the morning sunlight warm his body. Brandon plopped next to him and peered at the red and gray cliffs that towered over the city.

Eddie tossed a knapsack, a picnic basket, and a cooler in the front seat, climbed into the driver's side, and twisted to look at his passengers. "We're ready to start. I've got sodas and a meal packed for us, but there won't be many restrooms where we're going. If you need to stop, let me know."

Brandon's tenor sang in his ears. "I'm good."

"Me, too. But would you mind if we stopped at a Starbucks? I saw one a couple of blocks away. I'll spring for cappuccinos for all of us."

"Sure. I wouldn't touch that dreck that Annie keeps in the office either."

Rick couldn't suppress a chuckle. "Her name's really Annie? I was thinking she maybe took her style cues from old Annie Oakley movies."

"Hey, that's a good one, sir! Yeah, her real name's Annie, and you're right, she's a good ol' cowgirl. She can shoot a rabbit with a six-shooter from fifty feet. I've seen." He wheeled into the street. "You mind if I drop you off at the Starbucks and drive around the block? There won't be no place to park this time of day."

"Sure, no problem."

Rick hopped out of the car when Eddie paused in front of the store. Brandon climbed out, too. "I'll help you carry, Mr. Collier."

"Sure, thanks. But call me Rick, okay?"

Brandon's cheeks turned an endearing pink. "Yes, sir, uh, I mean, yes, Rick."

He grinned, and they joined the queue. "So, what kind of coffee would you like, Brandon?"

"Gee, I don't know. I usually fix whatever Peter has at home. French roast, I think."

"Well, they've got that here. I think I'll get an iced cappuccino. It's getting a little warm out there. How about you?"

"Sure, that sounds great. Thanks."

When they settled back in the jeep, Eddie eased into the tourist traffic. He spoke while he dodged between SUV's and jaywalking pedestrians. "My people have lived in this land for many generations. This is a holy place for us, one blessed by the Great Spirit."

Brandon still gripped the pamphlet he'd picked up in the office. "I read that this is one of four holy places in the world."

"Yes, that's true. There are four places where spiritual energies gather. Two of these vortexes have negative energy and two have positive. Sedona and Kauai, in Hawaii, are the two places with positive energy."

Rick smiled at the mention of vortices, or, as the locals seemed to prefer, vortexes. "How long have humans lived in his area, Eddie?"

"My people believe that humans came here eons ago from the underworld. Legends tell us they climbed vines from a deep hole and rose up here, in the center of the world. We call this place Wipuk, and some of us call ourselves Wipukpa. We have endured through three ages, and today we live in the fourth age."

Brandon nodded. "The hole in the ground...would that be Montezuma's Well, south of here? We drove by it on the way from Phoenix."

"That's the white man's name for it. When our people lived there, it was dry. But they sinned, and the Great Spirit brought the rains and the flood, and only two creatures emerged. Our people descended from the Lady of the Pearl, who was spared during the flood." He turned onto a gravel road and headed north. "We're going to Secret Canyon first. It'll be after eleven thirty when we get there, so we'll stop at the trailhead and have our lunch."

Rick leaned back and took in the red bluffs and ledges that towered over the valley. "This is such beautiful country. You're lucky that your ancestors came from such a wonderful place."

"The white man, he don't know where he came from. Someplace across the ocean, but he's forgotten his roots. The Wipukpa, we know where we come from. Right here."

Rick reflected on Eddie's words. *Lost roots. How true that is. What are my roots, anyway? Victoria's family has Lindermont Manor, but I'm an interloper even there. My family moved to Iowa from Wisconsin, and before that, no one knows or cares.*

Brandon leaned forward, and the sun gleamed in his eyes. "So, what do you do when you're not giving tours, Eddie?"

"I'm a student, sir."

"Wow, really? Me, too! I want to be a doctor. What are you studying?"

"I'm working on my master's degree in geology."

"So you know all about what made these canyons, and the bluffs, and everything? Tell us!"

Rick slit his eyes against the sun and listened. *Ah, to be young again, when the world is new and fresh.*

"You see how the mountains rise in sheer cliffs above the canyon?"

Brandon nodded and craned his neck to peer overhead.

"The red strata that you see exposed are from the Schnebly Hill formation. It's found only in Sedona and is over two hundred and eighty million years old. It was laid down in the Permian, when this area was a swamp and the Rocky Mountains uplift hadn't started. The cream-colored layers on top are the Coconino Sandstone, the bones of dunes from a desert that was here after the swamp. Even later, when the mountains came, wind and water eroded out the softer parts of the sandstone and left the canyons you see today."

Brandon pointed to peaks in the distance. "But those mountains over there are a different color. They're all gray."

"They're made of Hermit Shale. They came from another swamp, about a hundred million years later. This is an ancient land, and living things from many eons have left their mark." His fingers reached into his knapsack and he pulled out a rock that he passed to the backseat. "Here's a fossil I found in the high desert last year."

Brandon turned the russet stone over and over in his hands. "Wow, it's a huge insect." He held it out to Rick. "Look! You can see the veins running through its wings and the segments of its body."

"It's pretty neat." He handed it back to Eddie. "Can you tell us more about how your people came here?"

"If you mean the science, archeologists say my people have been here at least four thousand years, maybe longer."

"I was more interested in the story of the flood."

"We're almost to where we'll stop for lunch. I'll tell you then. Enjoy the scenery, meantime."

Before long, the jeep bounced into a gravel parking lot. Eddie climbed out and spread a blanket with brilliant Apache designs on the scraggly grass. "Help yourself to drinks and food in the picnic basket. I brought sodas and Indian tacos. They should still be hot, so dig in."

Rick looked at the cliffs that loomed overhead and at the Ponderosa pines scattered on the hills. "This place is wonderful, Eddie. You said it's called Secret Canyon?"

"Yeah. It's kind of off the beaten path. If you ever need a place to be alone, to think, this is it. Not many people come here." He strode over to what looked like a vending machine mounted on a post and fed it coins.

Brandon popped a can of diet soda and called to him. "What's that, Eddie? It's not a slot machine, is it?"

A smile creased Eddie's features. "No, the Indian casino is on the freeway, to get the tourists. This is for our hiking permits. They're required to follow these trails." He handed a ticket to each of them. "Keep them. They're good for a week."

Rick relaxed on the blanket and took a bite from a taco. "These are delicious. Thanks for taking care of us." The scent of juniper and cedar wafted from the forest. Nearby, a yucca tree extended its spines heavenward while a Manzanita bush huddled underneath. A scattering of yellow and purple wildflowers bloomed in the grayish-green desert grasses that covered the slope above their picnic site.

"Glad to, sir. It's all part of the fee." He folded his legs into a criss-cross position and joined them in their meal. "Now, would you like to hear my people's creation story?"

"You bet!" Brandon sprawled on his back and stripped off his T-shirt. "Mind if I get some rays while you talk? It's a beautiful day." His muscles rippled in the sunlight, and the toasting of auburn hair on his chest glistened in the golden glow. An enticing trail of dark bristles traced over his washboard abdomen and ended in his blue jeans. A necklace made from links of steel, fastened with a small brass padlock, clung about his neck and flashed sunlight in Rick's eyes.

More than the magnificent vistas that surrounded them, this vision of male perfection took Rick's breath away. He tried not to stare, but couldn't withdraw his gaze. *No one should have hips that narrow and shoulders that broad.*

Eddie looked from one to the other of his companions, and a smile toyed with this lips.

Rick caught his expression from the corner of his eye and managed to return his attention to their guide. "So, can you tell us the story?"

"I told you how my people lived in Montezuma's Well, before it was a lake." Eddie's calm tones lulled the desire that boiled just under the surface of Rick's flesh. "When the Great Spirit filled it with waters, only two creatures emerged: the Lady of the Pearl and a woodpecker. The Lady was trapped inside a log and floated in the waters. After forty days and forty nights, the rain stopped and the log came to rest here, in Wipuka. The woodpecker freed her, and she was so beautiful that the Sun fell in love with her and took her for his wife. She gave birth to the First Lady, the ancestress of all my people. If we are lucky, we will see a woodpecker on the trail today."

Rick nodded. "That's a lovely story. Why was she called the Lady of the Pearl? There aren't any pearls here, are there?"

Eddie reached into a pocket and pulled out a quartz crystal. "This is a pearl. The Great Spirit gave us two stones with the power to protect our spirits. The white stone protects our women, and the blue stone, turquoise, protects our men." He pulled a leather pendant from under his shirt and showed them the turquoise embedded in silver. "This is a gift from the one I love to protect me from evil. I wear it always."

Brandon sat up and hugged his knees. "That's beautiful." His fingers toyed with the padlock at his neck. "I wish someone cared enough to give me something like that."

Rick's heart ached at the loneliness and yearning in the young man's voice. *I wish someone cared for me that way, too.* The thought startled him, and it scared him as well.

Eddie reached out and grasped each of their hands. The wind billowed about them, and his ponytail fluttered behind him like a raven in flight. Brandon's red hair flamed over his head as though he were afire. Rick's shorter locks blew across his forehead and clouded his vision.

Eddie's gentle voice wafted through the breezes to their ears and beyond. "If you listen to the Great Spirit, he will lift up your souls with his wisdom. Sometimes, when the Sun warms our bodies, he reaches out and gives two people love, just as the Sun found love with the Lady of the Pearl. When the Great Spirit speaks, listen with all your heart and you will find your deepest, most secret desires fulfilled." He closed his eyes and held them joined together for a few seconds. Magnetism flowed from his grasp and swirled about inside Rick's head.

Eddie loosened his grip, gathered up the wrappings from their tacos, and threw them in the trash. He returned to the jeep and pulled a digital camera from his pack. "One more thing. I want to take a picture of the two of you." He pointed to the trailhead. "Stand over there."

Brandon grinned and leaned on the Park Service sign while Rick strode to the other side.

Eddie shook his head. "No, that's no good. The sun's wrong. Stand over here." He took them by the hand and led them next to a Manzanita bush abloom with flowers. He peered through the viewfinder. "Stand closer. Brandon, put your arm over Rick's shoulder. Smile for me. That's it! One more." He grinned and slipped the camera in a pocket. "We'll mail you prints in a week or so." He pointed down the trail. "Let's head out. After we do the trail here, we still have to go to Cathedral Rock. There's a vortex there, and we need to be there at sunset to feel its full power."

* * * *

As they approached Cathedral Rock on Back O'Beyond Road, the sun hung low in the western sky, an enormous orange ball that hovered just above the cliffs. Long shadows fell across the valley and promised to cool the afternoon. Rick's joints creaked when he climbed out of the jeep and eyed the trail. In front of him, red-orange spires towered into the waning sunlight.

"It really does look like a cathedral," he whispered.

Eddie nodded. "It's a sacred place. We should hurry if we're going to make it to one of the saddlebacks in time to see the sunset. The vortex isn't far from where we'll stop."

Brandon bounced out of the jeep and gazed at the mountain formations. "They look kind of like obelisks with knobby tops." He grinned. "I guess I won't say what *that* reminds me of."

He turned a deep crimson, from his face all the way down to his exposed chest.

Rick glanced back at the spires and chuckled at the phallic images. "You know, you're right. I'm surprised none of the tour books mention that! I guess that'd be too X-rated."

Eddie frowned. "Follow me. The trail is steep in places, so please be careful. "He glanced at Brandon. "You may want to take your shirt along. It'll get chilly pretty quickly, once the sun goes down."

Brandon stuffed his T-shirt into the right side of his blue jeans. "Sure. Thanks for the hint. Lead on!"

Rick followed last, not the least so that he could watch the intricate play of the muscles on Brandon's back as he strode along the trail. Rick's body ached from the unaccustomed strain of the day's hikes, but the sight of that lithe form energized him. He hitched at his pants to hide his incipient erection. *Goddamn. Watch yourself. What the fuck are you thinking, anyway?* he chided himself. *You made your choices ages ago. It's too late for you now.*

They scrambled up the steep trail, at one point crawling on all fours to make it to the top.

Soon they stood in a saddleback on a sandstone ledge between two of the spires. The dying sun glared in their eyes.

Eddie pointed to two nearby rugged steeples of stone. "If you look at those just right, you can see that they resemble two people with their backs to each other. Legend is that they were a couple who lived in the valley long ago. They fought with one another and the Great Spirit told them to heal their differences or their hearts would turn to stone. They didn't listen, and today they are frozen here, in the rocks."

Rick stared at the formations and thought of Victoria. *Hearts to stone. How appropriate. It's just like the story of our marriage.* He sighed, crouched on the sandstone plate, and stared at the sunset while gloom and guilt gripped his mind.

Brandon settled next to him, and their arms brushed against one another. Desire flared deep within Rick for a moment. But then sorrow welled in his soul. He yearned to hold this young innocent, and for those strong arms to embrace him, to find solace for his sins in that beating heart. *Not to be, not to be. You get what you deserve in life, and I don't deserve that.*

Overhead ravens circled and laughed at the absurdity of existence. The sun disappeared behind the distant cliffs, and daylight perished while they watched. In the valley below, Oak Creek slithered through the dark greenery, a silvery snake that glowed in the faint light.

Eddie pointed to a pyre of black lava rocks nearby. "The vortex centers there. If you are still, its power will flow through you and give you the energy for whatever you desire."

Rick cast a forlorn glance at the silent rocks. *If only it were so simple.* He let his arm graze against Brandon's one last time and closed his eyes against his unshed tears.

Chapter Four

"Someone to Watch Over Me"

Brandon pulled the rented Audi sports car into the driveway and let a broad smile crease his features. He jumped out and sang an off-key duet with his iPod, warbling "Someone to Watch Over Me" with Michael Feinstein. The sun toasted his back through his sleeveless T-shirt, and the wind fluttered through his hair. He opened the car's minuscule trunk and heaved two overflowing sacks of groceries into his arms. He'd put on his shortest shorts this morning. Peter liked the way they clung to his narrow hips and exposed the muscles that flexed under the thick hair on his legs, but now the Manzanita bushes in Madonna's landscaping scraped against his shins. He shrugged, too filled with happiness to care. The clean scents of pine and juniper mingled with the perfume of the rosebuds in their arbor. A rainbow of periwinkles blossomed around the patio.

He fumbled the back door open with one hand and plopped the groceries onto the kitchen counter. His off-key duet with his iPod continued as he returned outdoors and pulled another sack of groceries from the trunk. He took special care with a small package covered with bright blue gift wrapping and adorned with a brilliant red bow.

"Peter! Honey, I'm home!" Brandon put the last sack of groceries on the counter along with the package. *He must be watching television, the dear. He's kind of hard of hearing sometimes.* While he stored the groceries his gaze lingered on the gift-wrapped package with its bow, and a silly grin played across his features.

When the food was all stored in the larder, he pulled a recipe book from the shelf in the pantry. He opened it to the page he'd marked earlier in the day and laid out the ingredients for the twice-cooked pork dinner he planned to fix for this evening. *Peter loves Asian food. This will be a special surprise for him.*

He prepared the marinade, chopped and ground fresh ginger and garlic, and mixed in the hoisin sauce and the sesame seed oil. The odors of the herbs and spices mixed with the Gershwin melodies that filled his ears. Feinstein was crooning now about "The Man I Love." *How cool is that? Just like me.* Once he sliced the pork into thin strips and mixed it with the marinade, he picked up the gift, dropped his iPod on the kitchen table, and went looking for his lover.

"Peter, where are you?" The mansion had its own little theater for watching movies, but he wasn't there. He passed through the living room and the game room, but still no Peter. "Where are you, sweetheart?" *Maybe he's taking a nap in our room. I should be quiet.* He crept up the stairs and peeked through the door to the master suite.

Peter was there, naked on the bed, along with a muscular young man dressed all in white.

Brandon's breath caught in his throat, and his heart stopped. *Oh my God! Is he hurt? Is that a medic from an ambulance?* "Peter! Are you all right?"

Then he looked closer. The guy's hands stroked Peter's back, and the strong scent of wintergreen wafted his way. He was getting a massage from a professional masseur.

Peter twisted his head and stared at the door. "There you are. Took you long enough to get back from the store." He pointed to an empty glass on his nightstand. "Be a dear and get me another gin and tonic, would you? I think Tony could use something, too."

Brandon's breath quavered in his throat. "A gin and tonic?"

Peter reached out and waggled his glass. "Don't forget to crush the ice."

He bit his lip and stared at the masseur. "I could have given you a backrub if you wanted one, Peter."

"Tony's a professional. And my old sciatica was acting up, so I gave him a call. He took a cab here, but when he's done you'll need to give him a ride back into town." He stuck out his glass and scowled. "Now get me my drink, please. And one for Tony, too."

Tony's British accent sounded like something from a bad James Bond movie. "I'll have a gin martini, if you don't mind." He still hadn't bothered to look at Brandon. "Shaken, not stirred. And easy on the vermouth."

Brandon hid the gift behind his back as he reached for Peter's glass, but the older man's eyes snapped on to it like an eagle swoops onto a desert rat. "What's that?"

"Nothing. Just a little something I picked up for you in town. You can open it later."

"Whatever. Leave it on the dresser while you fix our drinks, will you?"

Brandon took the empty glass and retreated to the bar in the living room downstairs. He stood and pressed his palms against his eyes while his breath caught in his throat. *I'm being selfish. He deserves a professional rubdown if he wants one.* He opened his eyes and gazed at the sun streaming into the living room from the patio. The warm, redwood paneling and the Navajo area rugs should have provided welcome comfort, but sickness fouled his stomach and his lips tugged downward on his face.

He blinked back tears and inspected the bar's refrigerator. "No olives, no limes," he muttered. Back in kitchen, he found each in the refrigerator. When he sliced the lime, the knife slipped in his trembling hands and nicked his thumb. "Shit." A drop of blood beaded on the cutting board. He sucked on the wound and turned to the sink. He ran cold water on it and then pressed it with a paper towel. *I'll get a Band-Aid later.* He returned to the bar with the olives and lime slices in a small crystal bowl.

He fixed the martini first, putting in extra vermouth and stirring it instead of shaking it.

With Peter's drink, though, he took care, almost like a priest consecrating the Eucharist. The clean scent of the gin and lime calmed his nerves. When he was finished, he took a sip to make sure the flavor was perfect, then wiped the glass to erase the signature of his lips.

On reluctant feet, he trudged back up the stairs. He had left the bedroom door open, but it must have drifted closed in a passing breeze. *Strange. I didn't think the windows were open.* He put the glass with the gin and tonic on a table in the hallway and opened the door. What he saw inside made him gasp, and he dropped the martini glass. It shattered against the marble flooring and splashed gin and vermouth on his legs.

Tony was giving Peter a blow job.

"Shit." He fell to his knees and pulled off his T-shirt, using it to wipe up the spilled drink and to gather the broken glass. A drop of blood oozed from his thumb where he'd cut it. "I'm sorry. I didn't mean to disturb you...."

Peter grunted and sat up. "It's all right. I was done." He cast an indifferent gaze at the mess on the floor. "I hope that's not my drink."

"No, no," Brandon stammered. "Yours is here, on the hallway table." He left his shirt in a soggy mess on the floor and strode across the room to hand Peter his drink. "Let me clean up. Tony, I'm sorry. I'll fix you another one in a minute."

"Oh, he can fix his own, now that I'm done with him." Peter waved his hand in dismissal at the masseur. "The bar's in the living room downstairs. I don't know why they don't have one in the bedroom, like sensible people." He slouched into a robe.

Tony stood as if to leave, but then he hesitated. "Uh, the hourly rate for services...."

"Tish and tosh." Peter set his drink down and grabbed his wallet. Without a glance at the amount, he pulled a wad of bills out. "Here. Is that enough?"

Tony counted them. "Yes sir, that's quite satisfactory. I'll just wait downstairs then."

Peter nodded. "Good. Brandon will take you back to town in a moment." He smiled at his young companion and patted the bed. "Now, you said you had a gift for me?"

Brandon shook his head and tried to stop the room from spinning. "Uh, yes." He stumbled to the dresser and handed the package to Peter. "I really need to clean this mess up. I don't want you stepping on broken glass."

Peter tore at the gaudy paper while Brandon gathered the remains of the martini goblet inside his T-shirt and dumped both the shards and his shirt in the trash. He slumped next to Peter while the older man opened the box that had been inside the gift wrapping. His thick hands pulled out the turquoise and silver medallion that Brandon had picked out that morning at a Navajo jeweler's studio in town.

Peter held it by two fingers, and his lips curled. "What is this...thing?"

"It's a medallion. The Indians believe that turquoise is a gift from the Great Spirit to guard men from evil. This one's a special design to protect the love that two people share."

"Well, it's grotesque. I hope you didn't spend too much money on it." He tossed it on the bed, where it landed on his spent condom.

"I used my allowance. I didn't spend any of your money."

"It's all my money, dear. Anyway, you got robbed." He gulped down his drink. "I think I'm going to relax in the sauna for a while. Why don't you return it and get your money back when you take Tony to town?" He meandered away toward the master bath.

* * * *

Brandon reflected that the little sports car and Eddie's jeep weren't made for the same roads. The Audi crunched and scraped bottom when he pulled into the parking lot for Secret Canyon. *If I wreck it, it'll just be another reason for him to be nasty to me.* He sighed and stared at the red bluffs on each side. *Over a thousand feet high,* Eddie's voice echoed in his head.

Yesterday seemed so far away. Yesterday he had been happy.

"God, I'm a mess." He glanced at the digital clock and wondered where the time had gone. It was hours ago that he'd dropped Tony off in town, hours he'd spent driving aimlessly, unwilling to return to face Peter. Dust caked his features, except for the streaks that tears had left when he'd stopped to weep. The dead weight of the medallion tugged at his shorts where it rested in his pocket.

One other car rested in the parking lot, a late-model Honda, but no one else was in sight. *Eddie told us this was off the beaten path. Just what I need.* He climbed out, squinted at the afternoon sun, and rubbed his bare chest. *I should have grabbed a shirt before I left.* He looked at the trailhead and thought about facing people. *Fuck it. Who cares if I get sunburned. Or cold. No one, that's who. I just need to be alone.* He strode off into the wilderness of Secret Canyon.

The trail twisted and turned through the valley floor, following an old roadbed. Prickly-pear cacti littered the canyon, while the red and gray cliffs soared overhead. The farther he hiked into it, the narrower the canyon got. He paused and ran his fingers over the lizardlike bark of an alligator pine and remembered hiking here yesterday. Memories of Rick, the shadow of his smile, the timbre of his voice, the golden brown of eyes, all these embraced him. Then he thought of Peter, his beloved Peter, getting a blow job. "From a fucking *prostitute.* How could he?"

He shut off his mind and emotions and concentrated on nature. At a fork in the trail, he turned left and the pathway climbed amid the Ponderosa pines. Before long, he was high over the narrow canyon, looking down a sheer face into the depths below. Red algae pooled like blood in the rivulets of the almost dry stream. An occasional Manzanita bush blossomed with pale, yellow flowers.

The trail turned a corner and he spied someone ahead of him, a man, who stood at the ledge and gazed at the vista below. Brandon frowned and started to turn away, but then looked back. His trim torso, his chestnut hair flecked with gray; that was familiar. He peered and certainty flooded through him. It was Rick, from yesterday, as beautiful as ever. Hesitation gripped him, and longing too. *I know he's supposed to be straight, but I could have sworn my gaydar lit up yesterday. When we sat together, and his arm brushed mine, I felt something, almost like we were meant for each other.* Peter's face flashed through his mind, and he recalled it contorted in pleasure this afternoon as Tony gave him a blow job. Rick's image turned blurry, and he blinked back tears. *I could sure use some companionship. He was so nice to me yesterday on the tour, almost like he cared about me. At the very least, maybe we can sit together for a while, like we did at Cathedral Rock last night. I felt so close to him then.*

He edged forward to better take in the other's profile. *His nose has that little bend in it, like a sculpture of Adonis. I wish he and I...I don't know what I wish.* As he neared, Rick shifted his position, almost as if he intended to leap off the precipice. A sudden scrabble of rocks slipped loose from underneath his feet, and he teetered on the edge.

Brandon surged forward, grasped him by the arm, and jerked him back to safety.

"Careful, there! Don't fall!"

Rick stumbled backward, lost his balance, and fell into his arms. The sunlight glinted in his eyes and a wild, shocked expression flared across his features. He stared at Brandon, and the color drained from his face. "You! What are you doing here?" He jerked himself away.

Brandon peered at him. "Are you all right? I was just hiking, and there you were. It looked like you lost your balance, so I grabbed you."

"I think I'm okay," Rick stammered. "Yeah, I guess that must be it. I lost my balance. I shouldn't have been standing so close to the edge." A shudder rippled through his body. "Thank you. I think you saved my life." He shook his head and took a deep breath. "I'm so sorry. I shouldn't have yelled at you." His trembling hands brushed loose grasses and dirt from his slacks and his jacket.

"You should be more careful. I'm just glad I was here." Brandon stood back and eyed him. "Are you sure you're all right?" *Those can't be tear streaks I see. Not on his face!*

Rick averted his eyes. "Yeah, yeah, I'm fine. I just feel like an idiot."

"Well, it could happen to anyone. You know, I guess there's a reason the guidebook says not to hike alone."

"Yeah. I knew it wasn't smart. I just needed to get away, you know? Be alone. And Eddie said this was the place to go." At last, those brown eyes rose to gaze at him. "Thank God you were here for me." He glanced around the empty forest. "Are you alone, too?"

"Yeah. Don't tell the rangers. They'll give us both a ticket."

Rick's eyes narrowed as he inspected Brandon's features. "How about you? Are you all right? You look like you've been...I mean...you look upset." He turned his eyes away.

Brandon remembered the tear-streaked dirt that blotted his image in the car mirror and wiped at his face. "Yeah, well, Peter and I kind of had a fight. It's nothing. I just needed to get away for a while and be alone. To think." He beamed, but his voice held a tiny tremor. "Just like you."

"You want to talk about it?"

"No. It all seems so silly now. I mean, you almost died, and that makes our tiff seem so trivial." He looked around and shivered. "Would you mind if we just sat for a bit, like we did at Cathedral Rock last night? I'd really like that."

"Sure. I need to catch my breath." He peeled off his jacket and handed it to Brandon. "Here. It's going to get cold when the sun sets."

He slipped into it, pulled it tight, and sat Indian-style on the ground. "Thanks. I don't know what I was thinking, running off without even my shirt. I was just...well, never mind."

He patted the soil next to him. "Just sit by me, okay? Like last night?"

Rick settled next to him, and their arms brushed once more. Brandon felt a thrill of electricity at that touch and wondered if it was deliberate. They rested in silence while the winds whistled in the trees and a coyote sang a lonesome song from a distant hill. He thought of their happy time together the day before and, on a sudden impulse, reached into his pocket and pulled out the turquoise medallion. "Here." He handed it to the other man. "I'd like you to have this."

Rick's eyes widened, and he held it like it was the most precious jewel he'd ever seen. "This is beautiful, Brandon. I don't deserve this. You should give it to Peter."

"No." He didn't want to talk about Peter, not now, and not to Rick. "I want you to have it. It'll protect you from evil." He grinned. "Just stay away from the edges of cliffs, okay?" He fought against sobs that threatened to bubble from this throat.

Rick slipped it over his neck. "I'll wear it always. Thank you." He reached out and touched Brandon's cheek. "I'm twice over in your debt. How can I ever repay you?"

His chin trembled as he stared into those deep, brown eyes. "Don't be mad. But I could really use a hug right now, someone to make me feel warm and safe. Could you do that, like you care for me?"

Rick's features softened into a sad smile. "Of course I care for you. You're my friend. I'm glad we got to know each other yesterday, and today you saved my life." He scrunched closer, and his arm circled around Brandon's back.

Brandon sighed, stretched out his legs, and rested his head on the other's strong shoulder. "Thank you. This is nice." He placed a palm on Rick's chest, and the beating heart in the other's breast pulsed against his hand.

Rick turned his head and looked down at him. His warm breath wafted across Brandon's cheek. "You're quite a young man, Brandon. Peter's very lucky to have you. I hope he treats you right." His voice was a whisper, a promise, a prayer.

Tears leaked once more onto Brandon's cheeks. He tipped his head up and stared into those brown eyes, so filled with compassion. He inhaled Rick's sweet scent and the world seemed to stop. For one magical instant, as if in a dream, their lips brushed together. In the waning light, he thought he glimpsed a tear glistening in the other's eye. He pulled back and gazed at that lovely face. "I wish..." he murmured.

"Yes?" That one word was so soft and deep that it sang a cantata of romance with Brandon's heart.

"I wish I had someone to watch over me." He sighed. *Someone like you. But I dare not say it.*

"That's someone I'm longing to see, too," Rick whispered, so faint the words floated away like smoke.

A cold wind gusted from the peaks, and they shivered. Rick stood. "We should get back before you freeze to death."

Chapter Five

"Stardust"
November 2008

Rick's fingers twisted at the stiff collar of his shirt. *Goddamned tuxedos, anyway. Why did I let Sandra talk me into coming to this thing?* He turned his back on the elite crowd at the Celestial Ball. He'd picked out a corner of the Sky Pavilion at the Adler Planetarium where he could gaze at the constellation of Chicago's city lights that glittered up the lake shore. "At least here I've got a good view, and I don't have to mingle with those snobs," he muttered.

He started as an arm slipped around his. Sandra whispered in his ear. "You know, it's not nice to abandon your date. We'll mingle together, and I'll do all the talking. It'll be good for you. You've not done anything but work since we got back from Sedona months ago. You can just stand there and look strong and handsome." She took a sip of her white wine, and her eyelashes fluttered at him.

He grimaced and pulled away. "Won't work. Everyone who knows me wants to ask me about the markets and the damned bailout. They should talk to their brokers instead of hitting me up for free financial advice."

"They're just making polite conversation." She gave his arm a gentle tug and turned him around to face the interior. "Look, isn't it lovely? This is one of my favorite benefits."

The sloping glass canopy and walls of the Pavilion arced away from them, lit by golden floor lamps. Gossamer strands of optical fiber hung from the glazing overhead and supported white cylinders that encased tiny spotlights. Colorful planetary globes made from acrylic dangled over their heads. A reporter's camera flashed, and the reflection of Saturn's rings gleamed for an instant in her eyes.

Rick glanced, not at the magnificent setting but at the throng attired in their best finery. He gulped at his bourbon on the rocks. "When does the dinner start?"

She grinned at him. "Soon. I know what you're thinking. There will only be six other people at our table, and that will limit your mingling to just them."

"Not a bad strategy, I think."

"This will be good for you. You really should get out more."

His lips turned down, and he gave her a dour look. "You know I've been busy. The market's been a mess. We've been repositioning ourselves for the last year, but it's still stressful."

"I'm sorry. I know you work hard. How's the fund holding up?"

"We'll be all right. We never did get into all those high-risk things, thank God. Victoria kept pressing us, but the Board sided with me."

"I remember."

A chime sounded, and an apologetic voice announced that the catering staff would serve dinner in ten minutes. Museum workers clutching clipboards wandered through the crowd and assisted people in finding their tables.

"I spoke to my friend Lydia about our seating. She's on the Women's Board, you know."

"What about our seating?"

"I pulled some strings. I think you'll be pleased with the others at our table."

He rolled his eyes. "Don't tell me you're trying to set me up with someone again." A vision of Lydia, with lips larger than Angelina Jolie's and a bust to rival Dolly Parton's, flashed in his mind, and he shuddered.

"No, I know better. I went for good conversation. I arranged for Peter Warren and his friend to sit with us."

A frisson of panic flashed through him as the memory of Brandon and their encounter in Secret Canyon echoed in his mind. He caught his breath, then muttered, "Warren's a jerk. Why did you do that?"

"Yes, he's unbearable. But I ran into him and his friend, Brandon, when we were in Sedona. We had lunch together while you were off doing some dreadful, boring thing—it might have been the day you drove up to look at that meteor crater, or maybe it was when you went by yourself on that silly jeep tour. I don't know. Anyway, Brandon is the most delightful young man. He's taking pre-med courses by correspondence. Isn't that just darling?"

"Yeah. Darling." Excitement fluttered in his stomach. *What will we say to each other? I wish...God help me, I don't know what I wish. Fuck, will he mention that kiss?* The thought of

Brandon's lips against his brought a terrifying thrill to his inner being that pulsed out his genitals. He slurped down the last of his bourbon and glared at Sandra. "Well, let's get it over with. What table are we at?"

"Table five. It's up front, so we can listen to that astronaut fellow's speech after dinner."

"Humph. I'd rather be in the back so we could sneak out."

"Now, now. Remember, I went to that awful gallery opening with you. You owe me. So be nice." She hooked arms with him, and they strolled through the crowd to their table.

They found an imposing young woman already seated at their table. She was in her middle thirties, with pale skin, raven-colored hair in a tight French curl, and crystalline blue eyes. Rick shook her hand and introduced himself and Sandra.

Her gaze seemed to penetrate his soul, and he felt she could read his mind. Her hand lingered in his, her voice deep and deliberate. "Montgomery Bank and Trust. A very respectable firm. Nice to meet you, Sandra, Rick. I'm Fran MacDonald."

Rick frowned. "Fran MacDonald. That name's familiar. I know! You were the defense attorney in that Alderman's murder trial. He was accused of killing his girlfriend and burying her body in Lincoln Park."

She smiled. "My reputation precedes me, I see. Yes, that was my case. We do criminal law, with a bit of corporate liability on the side. I'm the main litigator for our firm."

"How interesting!" Sandra gushed while her fingers squeezed Rick's arm. "You'll have to tell us all about your cases." She positioned herself with an empty chair between her and Fran and waited for Rick to seat her.

He gave her a grim little smile and pulled out the chair next to Fran for her to sit in.

"Sandra, do be seated. I see a client I need to say hello to. Excuse me, please." He waited for her to sit before he escaped. He chatted with one of the caterers, for cover, while he kept an eye on their table.

An older, heavyset man settled on Fran's left, and then another couple arrived. The man's belly seemed about to explode from his tuxedo, and wisps of white hair on his head floated over his red face. The woman wore a fortune in jewels about her neck and her fingers, and her body jiggled as she walked. They sat on the opposite side of the table from Sandra. *Thank God. I won't have to talk to them.* Then he realized that the only remaining seats would go to Brandon and Warren, and a black hole of anxiety contracted in his gut.

Warren finally swaggered up to the table, as repugnant and fat as he'd remembered. But Brandon wasn't with him! Instead, a young man with blond, spiky hair sat in the chair next to Peter. He, too, looked as if his tuxedo might explode, but this time from coiled muscles rather than corpulence. Rick peered in the dim light and noticed that the young man's hair had dark roots underneath the platinum tips. *He's good looking, in a trashy kind of way, I'll give him that. But where's Brandon?* He took his leave of the caterer and made his way to the table.

First he introduced himself to the older couple, and at once forgot their names. He turned to Warren and extended his hand.

"Peter, so nice to see you again. Rick Collier here, from Montgomery Trust."

Warren shook hands without standing. "Frederick Collier, yes, I remember you. Sorry I missed you in Sedona. I had a nice lunch with your charming sister-in-law."

Rick cocked an eyebrow at the blond interloper. "And who is your companion this evening, Peter?"

The young man jumped to his feet. "My name's Jude Johnson. Nice to meetcha, Freddy."

Rick didn't quite cringe. "Please, call me Rick." He withdrew his hand before Jude could finish crushing it, and it flexed his fingers. "It's a pleasure."

He settled into his seat, with Jude on his right and Sandra on his left. The caterers had prepositioned the salads, and he noticed that Jude had slathered his with dressing and already eaten a third of it. He cleared his throat and pointed to the carafe with the vinegar and oil. "I wonder, Peter, if you might pass the dressing this way?"

Sandra and Fran were engaged in an animated conversation about the election next week.

Don't want to get roped into that, not in this crowd. I bet Republicans outnumber us two to one tonight. Peter and the bejeweled woman were also chatting about politics, but from a somewhat different perspective than on his left. *Good thing those two groups can't hear each other, or we'd have a riot right here.* He picked at his salad and tried to make himself inconspicuous.

"So, Rick, what do you do for a living?" Jude chomped on his salad. On the way to his mouth, his fork had dribbled a trail of dressing on the tablecloth.

"I work at a bank, Jude. How about you?"

"Oh, I'm a dancer. I was working at Big Daddy's, up on Halsted, when I met Peter."

"Big Daddy's? I don't believe I know that establishment."

"It's a dive, a strip joint. But it paid good and gave me a chance to practice my moves. I'm gonna try out for that TV show. You know the one?"

"I'm afraid not. Perhaps you could fill me in?"

"It's like *American Idol*, 'cept it's for dancers. They have a dance-off every week, just like on *Idol*, and they eliminate the losers."

"It sounds exciting. Are you studying dance professionally? To prepare?"

"Oh yeah. Peter set me up with a dance coach. He's a ballet per-fessor at Northwestern, but he's good. He knows all the right moves. When the tryouts come to Chicago next year, I'll be ready. I've got the looks and the bod that the judges want. I'm gonna win me a trip to Vegas."

"It's so admirable that you have a goal, Jude."

"You betcha. I wanna dance for the shows in Vegas. Peter says he'll help set me up, after I win."

"Peter's very generous. How long have you known him?" Rick leaned back and let the server remove his salad plate. Other waiters brought the women their main courses.

Jude shoved his plate at a waitress. "We've been together almost six weeks. He was with some other guy before me, but Peter dumped him, or maybe it was the other way around. Anyway, Peter said he was a selfish little bitch."

"Really?" Rick couldn't imagine anyone calling Brandon selfish.

A server leaned over and murmured in his ear, "Chicken or veal, sir?"

He smiled and replied, "I'll have the chicken, thank you."

Jude's eyes bore into the server's face. "Hey bub, I want the veal." Jude didn't wait for the others and dug in as soon as he had his plate. Between gulps, he continued their conversation. "Peter told me this other guy, Bruce, Brian, something like that, I don't remember his name. Anyway, he said this other guy was way jealous and controlling and bitched him out all the time."

Sandra touched Rick's arm, and relief flooded through him as he turned to her. "You owe me big time for this," he whispered to her.

"Sorry, I didn't know he'd bring someone different," she muttered back. Then she raised her voice, "Rick, Fran tells me that the Chief Financial Officer at Axinon Investments has retained her as counsel. Don't you know him?"

He glanced at Sandra's neighbor and smiled. "Yes, Darren and I were at Northwestern at the same time, in the business school. I do hope he's not in any kind of trouble. You did say you specialized in criminal law?"

"Yes, that I do, Rick. I should have thought you'd heard about Axinon's problems." Fran's eyes snapped at him, as if probing for a confession like Perry Mason.

"I haven't seen Darren in months. I think perhaps we chatted at the symphony last spring. May I ask what's going on? Axinon has a good reputation. It's a bit risky for my taste, but its returns have been good."

Sandra chimed in. "The Feds are investigating Axinon. You remember Brian Steadman?"

Rick kept his face impassive. "Yes. Weren't the two of you on some boards together last year?" *More like they were in some beds together. Where's this leading, anyway?* He peered at Sandra, but her face gave no clue.

"Well, this Steadman was Chairman of Axinon's Board. And he disappeared, just like that, last February." Sandra nodded her head.

"February. Now that's a...."

Before he could say coincidence, Sandra kicked him under the table and interrupted, "Yes, isn't that strange? Apparently he said he was going on a vacation to Europe, but he just up and vanished, without a trace."

He frowned at her and rubbed his shin. *Just like Victoria. And the month before she took off, too. Sandra never did tell me why she and Steadman broke up. I wonder what's up?* He glanced back at Fran. "So, what does this have to do with my friend Darren?"

"Well, it's pretty strange that someone in Steadman's position disappeared. And now the SEC is investigating the firm—they've been auditing the books for over a year. The U.S. Attorney seized a bunch of their records last week." Fran patted her napkin on her lips. "I really can't comment much beyond what

Sandra said. But I have a feeling this is part of something much bigger. So does your friend Darren. That's why he hired me."

Rick frowned. "As I recall, Axinon was pretty heavy into hedge funds. But I thought they were hooked up with Bernard Madoff somehow. He's supposed to be sound, and his profit margins have been remarkable."

Fran nodded. "Yeah, remarkable. Unbelievably so, some would say. Does your bank have money in Madoff's funds?"

"No. He was never forthcoming enough for us to assess the risk, so we stuck with more conventional instruments. But we're pretty conservative in any case. Our returns haven't matched the big investment banks, but we haven't lost as much in the last few weeks either. In fact, we've done quite well, considering."

Sandra patted his hand. "Rick's a financial genius. If anyone can see the bank through the current mess, it's him."

He smiled. "I'm afraid no one is going to come out of this unscathed. The next couple of years are going to be nasty, no matter who wins the election this week. But the bank does seem to be rather well-positioned."

Fran's companion turned to her with a question and left Rick with no choice but to rotate back in the direction of Jude and Warren.

Sandra threw a gleaming smile at them. "Peter, I so enjoyed our lunch in Sedona, what was it? Two months ago?"

"A little over that, my dear. Yes, we had a delightful time." Peter pushed his entree aside and took a large bite out of his chocolate cheesecake.

Rick caught a mischievous gleam in Sandra's eye as she asked, "Whatever happened to that charming young man you had with you on that trip? What was his name again?"

"Brandon. He left right after we returned to Chicago from that trip. Just took off. After all I did for him, too. I paid his tuition for college, and bought him a computer, a place to live, nice clothes. And I'd just taken him on that wonderful vacation. He just walked out without even a thank you. Quite an ingrate, I'm afraid. Serves me right, I suppose. Most boys would give their eyes to see the places I took him."

"Well, that would rather defeat the purpose, wouldn't it?" Rick purred.

Warren gave him a puzzled look.

"I'm glad he's gone," Jude declared. "Otherwise I would have never met my honey." He grinned and wrapped his arm around Warren's pudgy form.

Sandra *tsk*ed. "Seems such a shame. I thought he was a charming young man." Her fingers brushed at Rick's arm. "Do you have any idea what became of him?"

Rick smiled at the lilt in her voice. *She's taunting Warren.*

Peter snorted. "Really, I could care less. He was a low-class little cur. I imagine he went back to that south side tenement he grew up in."

Jude piped up. "Oh, Peter, we saw him! Don't you remember? At Nike Town, last week."

"What? Oh yes. That was unfortunate." Warren shook his head.

Jude turned to Rick and Sandra. "We ran into him when Peter got me new shoes last week."

"Really?" Rick took two small bites of his dessert and pushed it away.

"Yeah. I needed them for working out. For my dance lessons, you know. Anyway, this Brandon creep's a clerk at Nike Town, on Michigan Avenue. Can you believe that? What a fuckin' loser. A shoe clerk!"

"Who knew?" Rick didn't quite sneer. *Poor kid. That asshole Warren probably just kicked him out with nothing.*

"Hey, are you gonna eat that?" Jude pointed at Rick's discarded dessert.

"No, it's a bit rich for me, I'm afraid."

"Great. I love this stuff." Jude shoved his empty plate to one side and replaced it with Rick's. He proceeded to wolf down the remains of Rick's cheesecake.

Sandra leaned into him and whispered, "Gawd, where did Peter find him?"

"At a strip club up on Halsted."

Sandra looked like she might explode and pressed her napkin to her lips while her eyes twinkled at Rick.

He leaned back and sighed. *I just wish this evening would be over.* He thought about work tomorrow and reflected that Nike Town was just a few blocks from the bank, easy walking distance. *I guess I could use a new pair of sneakers.*

Chapter Six

"Come on-a My House"

Brandon stretched and gazed over the almost empty computer lab in the public library.

The clunk from the movement of the minute hand on the wall clock reminded him that if he didn't hurry, he'd miss the train. He sighed and slipped his unfinished homework into his spiral-bound notepad. He logged out of his correspondence course, stuffed his books into a plastic Wal-Mart bag, and scuttled out of the building and onto Belmont Avenue.

"At least the weather's still warm," he muttered as he rushed two blocks to the Red Line's elevated platform. He clutched at the light jacket he'd put on that morning to hide the striped referee's shirt that he had to wear at Nike Town. Once on the platform, he squinted up the tracks, looked for his train, then glanced at his watch. "Come on, come on. I can't be late."

When the train finally arrived, he scrambled on board and collapsed into a seat. *At least I beat the noon rush.* He pulled out his chemistry textbook and tried to read, but when the tracks descended into the tunnels after Fullerton Station, the flickering light and the rocking of the coaches defeated him. He dropped the book into his bag, leaned back, and closed his eyes. At the Chicago Street stop, he left the train and ran up the stairs to the street. He squinted at his watch and trotted the first couple of blocks on the way to Nike Town on Michigan Avenue.

The store still amazed him. When he pushed through the revolving doors, new age music washed over him and mingled with recorded crowd noises and the bustle of customers. Overhead, life-sized, plaster statues of mountain bikers hung from the ceiling of the three-story atrium, and banners that proclaimed *Performance, Technology, and Innovation* fluttered in artificial breezes. Everywhere displays and posters told the history of athletes or inspiring stories about overcoming adversity. It was more like a shrine to athletic shoes than a retail store.

As always, tourists jammed the place, and he edged his way through the ogling crowd to the employee lounge at the back. Once there, he clocked in and secured his coat and books in his locker. *Eight minutes to spare. Time enough for coffee.* He fed the vending machine and blew on the steaming brew while he inspected next week's schedule. "Damn." They had him working the weekend again. He'd counted on spending Saturday at the library, logged on and doing homework.

He gulped at the scalding liquid in his paper cup and made sure he had a supply of little Nike stickers with his sales ID number stamped on them. He didn't get a commission, but the store management did keep track of how many customers he helped. Part of his job included slipping these stickers on a customer's prospective purchases, so he'd get credit on his next evaluation for being productive and promoting store sales.

He sighed and returned to the retail floor. He took the main escalator to the level with the men's specialty shoes. When he got there, Sammy, his supervisor, glanced at his wristwatch and frowned.

"Ah, Brandon. Squeaking in just under the start of your shift again, I see."

I guess that translates to 'on time and good to see you' *in Sammy-speak.* Brandon flashed a smile at him. "Nice to see you, Sammy. How's business been today?"

"Lots of tourists still around from the big election celebration two nights ago at Grant Park. Great for business." Behind him, a rainbow of tropical fish swam in one of the aquariums that decorated the museum-like interior of the store. He turned, posed before his reflection in the glass, and primped his coal-black curls to tousled perfection. "Hop to it, my lad. The store's crawling with opportunity."

Brandon glanced at the poster of Michael Jordan that hung above the aquarium. A quote from William Blake adorned the image: *No bird soars too high, if he soars with his own wings.* It gave him hope that, maybe someday, he'd escape from this retail hell.

"Yes, sir. Right away," he muttered, and started to cruise for customers. *Just like the bars right before closing,* he mused. *Everyone's looking for a hook-up.*

He spotted an overweight, middle-aged woman with big, peroxide hair and too much makeup who was puzzling over the selection of weight-training shoes. "Good afternoon, ma'am. Can I assist you?" Brandon beamed at her.

"Why yes, you may. I wondered if this place had any help." She held up two different shoeboxes. "I'm thinking of getting one of these for my husband. He works out at the Y in Willamette, and his birthday is coming up."

"Yes, ma'am, I'll be happy to assist you. All of these shoes are designed for the needs of people who lift weights. They won't catch on the equipment, and they give extra support to the arches and ankles from the stresses of lifting weights."

"But what's the difference between these two?"

About seventy dollars, Brandon thought, but he continued with his spiel and described the features of each shoe in detail.

She frowned. "I don't know. It's a lot of money. Couldn't he just buy regular running shoes? He jogs on the track after he works out, you know."

"Well, ma'am, that's good to know. These could work for jogging, but that's a different set of stresses on the body. Maybe you'd like to see some of our jogging shoes, too?"

"How far away are they? I'm pretty sick of looking at men's shoes." Her ample bosom heaved with an enormous sigh. "Shopping is such hard work...." She looked around and plopped her copious fundament on a nearby bench. "I'll just wait here, and you bring them to me."

He glanced at the shoes she'd been looking at. "I take it you'd like something in orange?"

"Yeah, he's a big Fighting Illini fan. Orange and blue, if you've got it."

"I'm sure I can find something. I'll be right back." He paused and eyed the other sales staff. "Are you sure you wouldn't like to come with me? That way I won't have to guess what you might like."

She scowled at him. "I said I was tired. If it's too much trouble, I'll ask that nice man over there." She nodded at Sammy, who stood and watched their conversation with a hawk's eye.

"No trouble at all, ma'am."

He rushed off, hoping no one would steal his customer. He grabbed several pairs of jogging shoes, taking care to match color and size to the woman's needs. He juggled them in both hands and wove his way back to where she had been sitting, only to find her talking to Sammy.

Her voice twanged over the Muzak and buzz of other customers. "Thank you so much, young man. You've been very helpful." She glanced over as Brandon arrived. "There you are. I've decided to get the weight-training shoes after all. I can always come back and get jogging shoes later."

Sammy's discrete fingers slipped a Nike sticker with his sales ID onto her purchase before he handed it to her. "Here you go, ma'am. They can check you out on the first floor." He gave her his best salesman smile, his whitened teeth gleaming in his mouth. Brandon thought he looked like a shark preparing for the first bite.

As soon as her back was turned, Sammy wheeled to Brandon and winked. "Another easy sale. All you need to do is persuade them to buy what they've already picked out, not sell them something else." He pointed to the boxes in Brandon's hands. "Be sure to put those back before you return to the sales floor. And remember what I just told you. You'll do better."

Brandon scowled at his boss's back, but he trudged to the shelves and restocked the shoes. *Kind of like a library. Except I guess it pays better than reshelving books.* He longed for the solitude of his studies, but instead returned to the floor, dreading the demanding push of customers and the competition with the other sales staff. He sighed. *The noon-hour rush isn't even over yet...*

A hand tugged at his sleeve. "Excuse me; I wonder if you might help me?" The voice, a pleasing baritone, was familiar.

Brandon turned, and an electric thrill of recognition flickered through him. "Rick. I mean, Mr. Collier. Yes, of course I can help you." He balled his hands into fists to hide the sudden tremor that quivered in them.

Rick's dazzling smile swamped all the retail glitz and glitter. "Brandon. How nice to see you. And I told you to call me Rick, remember?" His eyes wrinkled at the corners and sparkled, whether reflecting the electric lights or an inner joy at this chance encounter Brandon couldn't say.

"Yes, Rick." They shook hands, and the other's strong touch thrilled his arm and sent a tingle down his spine. "So, can I help you find something?"

"Sure, but can we maybe catch up first? Unless you're in a hurry to do something else?"

"No... It's just...." He stammered and took a deep breath. "No hurry. It's been, what, almost four months since we last saw each other?"

"Yes. I confess I've thought of you often. You saved my life there in Secret Canyon. I haven't forgotten." His hand lingered in Brandon's, as if reluctant to break their renewed connection.

Brandon's face heated. "It was nothing." He glanced at Sammy, who was busy helping another customer. "I've thought about you, too. How have you been?" He wanted to ask if Rick's wife had returned, but couldn't think of a polite way to do it.

"Same old, same old. Things have been hectic at the bank, what with the financial situation. But we're doing fine." At last their hands parted, and his eyes took on a sad glint. "Lonely, too, I'm afraid. You knew my wife disappeared last spring? I haven't lived alone in years. It takes getting used to." He shook his head. "I heard about you and Peter. I'm so sorry. That must have been difficult for you."

Brandon frowned. "Not really. I thought we were in love, but he had other ideas. I'm much better off without him, really. Anyway, a boyfriend right now would just get in the way of my studies."

"Pre-med, as I recall. How's that going?"

"Well, my classes are all online, so it doesn't interfere with working here. I hang out at the library a lot to use their computers. It's tough, finding time, but I'm doing okay."

Rick's gaze raked him from head to toe. "I will say you're looking...healthy." He fingered his chin and smiled. "I like the whiskered look. Or did you just forget to shave this morning?"

Brandon chuckled. "The woman who cuts my hair suggested it. She called it a scruff beard. I use clippers with a guard every couple of days to keep it looking fresh. You don't think it makes me look too rough, do you?"

"I think it fits you fine."

Sammy bustled up to them and glared at Brandon before he threw a toothy smile in Rick's direction. "Is everything all right here, sir?"

"Yes, everything's fine." Rick nodded to Brandon. "I had lots of questions about running shoes. I'm just starting to jog, and your salesman has been quite helpful."

"Glad to hear it." He slapped Brandon on the back. "If you need anything, just let one of us know." He sauntered away to snag another victim.

Brandon's face heated once more with embarrassment. "God, I'm sorry. That's my boss's way of telling me to stop chit-chatting."

"Brandon, I'm so sorry. I didn't mean to get you in trouble."

"It's nothing I can't handle." He pulled a shoe at random from the shelf. "Here, just let me pretend to show you some shoes and he'll be happy."

Rick glanced at his watch. "It's really great to see you again, Brandon, but I've got an appointment back at the bank." He eyed the shoes. "Tell you what, I'll make a bargain with you. Give me something in a size 11D—anything—and I'll buy it. In return, will you have dinner with me? Is it a deal?" He pursed his lips. "I hope you don't think that's too forward, but I enjoyed our time together and

I'd like to reconnect with you. Plus, I owe you for saving me from falling into Secret Canyon."

Brandon's breath caught in his throat. "I'd like that, Rick. I'd like that a lot. But you don't have to buy any shoes."

"A deal's a deal. Tell you what; I'll whomp up something at my apartment. That way it'll be quiet, and we can get reacquainted without any distractions." It was Rick's turn to blush a deep crimson. "Unless you'd rather go out someplace public?"

Brandon tried to control the sudden heat that surged between his legs. "I'd be honored to call on you at your apartment, Rick. Just tell me when and where."

Rick's face flinched with a silly grin, and a bead of sweat trickled down his temple.

"Great! Get me some shoes to buy so your creepy boss will be happy." He pulled out a business card and scribbled on the back. "Here's my address and phone number. Shall we say seven, tomorrow night? Call me tonight, after eight, and I'll give you directions. It's a bit convoluted how to get there."

Brandon took the card and glanced at the address. "175 E. Delaware." He gave Rick a puzzled look. "That's just a couple of blocks north of here, right? But I don't recall any apartment complexes there."

"It's a unit in the John Hancock Center. I'll have to give you directions for the private elevators to the forty-fourth floor, then you'll have to pass the concierge at the reception area and elevators to the condos."

Brandon pulled a pair of black running shoes from the shelf. "The John Hancock Tower. I heard there were apartments there.

The views must be fantastic. I went to the observatory once, when I was a kid." He handed the shoes to Rick.

"Yeah, the view can be pretty spectacular. The condo was a wedding gift from Victoria's parents." He inspected the shoes. "Don't forget to put your sticker on the box." He held it out so Brandon could stick the Nike wings with his sales ID on the carton. "Call me tonight. I'm really looking forward to this!" He strode away before Brandon could say another word.

"He's looking forward to dinner with me," he murmured. "*He's* looking forward to it!" He suppressed the desire to dance with joy.

"Excuse me, young man, do you have these in a twelve narrow?" A man with the skeletal frame of a long-distance runner brought him back to reality by tapping him on the shoulder and holding up a pair of shoes.

"I'll check for you, sir. Just a minute." While he knelt to look over the stock, he frowned.

Strange that Rick didn't even try on those shoes. It's almost like he wasn't really shopping at all. Or at least like he wasn't shopping for shoes.

Chapter Seven

"Isn't It Romantic?"

Rick stepped out of the shower and swiped the steam from the mirror. He ran his palm over his chin and decided to shave again. Halfway through, the razor snagged on his jaw and a bubble of blood oozed into the white foam. "Shit." He wiped at it and paused to stare at himself in the mirror. *Look at you, you old fool. You're as giddy as a girl on her first date.*

He flexed his chest and twisted his abs, pleased at the washboard muscles that rippled on his torso. *All those hours in the gym have some benefit, at least.*

He finished shaving without another nick, but an annoying trickle still flowed from his jaw. He tore off a shred of tissue paper and pressed it against the wound, where it stuck. Next came a spray of cologne, deodorant, then a pause to run his fingertips over his hard chest.

Brandon's chest is thick with hair, he mused, and wondered what it would be like for his smooth body to rub against Brandon's bristly one. His cock lurched in response. He touched himself for a moment, then his hands shuddered away. *Stop that. It's not a date. It's just a dinner.* Thoughts of ice cubes and Victoria percolated in his mind, and his desire fled.

He slipped into jockey briefs, applied styling gel to his hair, and worked with the heat from the blow-dryer and his brush to arrange his curls to tousled perfection. The flecks of gray marked his age, and he thought again about touching them up. But Sandra had assured him they looked sexy, and besides, it seemed so vain to color one's hair.

The turquoise medallion lay by the sink, its silver chain coiled on top of it, where he'd left it before his shower. He picked it up and looped it over his head. His fingers lingered on the amulet for a moment, recalling that day in Hidden Canyon, so long ago and so far away, when Brandon had given it to him. "I've worn it every day, just like I promised," he whispered.

He slipped his Rolex over his wrist, noting the time. *No need to rush, but still, it can't hurt to get things ready.* Thinking of early birds and worms, he picked out a crisp, white shirt and a pair of navy-blue chinos. He glanced at the three brand-new pairs of Nikes that he'd bought this week. *Took me four lunch hours to find Brandon.* He grinned, remembering how he'd figured out the significance of the numbered Nike wings on his shoeboxes. He slid into penny loafers without bothering with socks and checked himself out in the mirror one more time. *It'll have to do, I guess.* He rolled his cuffs up to mid-arm and strode to the kitchen.

He started the sushi rice in the cooker, then peeled and sliced a cucumber and an avocado and placed them in a salad bowl. He added shredded carrots and scallions and strips of nori. When the rice was done, he fluffed it over the steamer and added it to the salad along with thin slices of crab. Finally, he mixed the wasabi, rice vinegar, and other ingredients for the dressing, tossed it into the salad, and garnished the whole thing with sesame seeds and more shredded seaweed. He grinned. *I wonder if Brandon's ever had sushi?* He stashed the whole thing in his refrigerator and wiped his hands on a towel.

The clock on the microwave read six thirty when the doorbell rang. He rushed to open it and greeted the delivery girl from the market on the forty-fourth floor. "Hi, Marie. Good to see you tonight. How have you been?"

"Great, Mr. Collier. Entertaining tonight, are you?" She handed over the warm packages of seafood and the box from the bakery.

"Just a little dinner I'm fixing, nothing special. How's that boyfriend of yours? Mark, right?"

She dimpled. "He popped the question last week." She held out her hand, where a diamond glittered on her ring finger.

"Marie!   That's   wonderful. Congratulations!" He reached into his wallet and handed her some bills. "Here's a little something extra. Go out and celebrate with him. And you better not forget to invite me to the wedding."

"Thanks, Mr. Collier. Don't worry, we'll remember you."

"You'd better! Thank Mr. Kikuchi for me, too, will you? I know it was extra service for him to steam and shell the lobster and shrimp for me, and I won't forget him."

"I'll tell him. He was glad to do it. He likes you too, Mr. Collier. Everyone likes you. Have a good time tonight. Don't do anything I wouldn't do. See you!" She dimpled at him again and turned away.

He placed the seafood on the counter and pulled the Sacre torte from the box, putting it on the sideboard next to the dining table. After a rushed glance at the clock, he set the table with pure white china and leaded crystal. He'd pressed and folded the cloth napkins into little Bishop miters the night before and placed those on top of the plates. He'd thought about using the good silver, but settled instead on the Danish stainless.

He stepped back and surveyed the room. Everywhere he looked, he saw the stamp of Victoria's cultivated taste. Her interior designer had framed the corner windows to match the angled exterior joists of the building. That was where she placed the glass dining table, huddled under the oblique walls. From there, her guests had a view of the lake on the right and the North Shore on the left. The designer set the polished planks of dark, mahogany flooring at an angle to the walls, drawing the eye to the windows and the dining table. Spotlights shined onto the space from a soffit in the ceiling. The walls were ivory, and she had insisted on a black Corbusier sofa, Wassily chairs, and marble coffee table for the sitting area. One of Victoria's paintings, an abstract landscape, provided a splash of vibrant color. He dimmed the lights in the rest of the room, hoping to create an intimate corner for dining. *I guess that'll have to do. I wish it were homier. Victoria's style is so damned pretentious.*

The doorbell chimed again, and an electric thrill ran through him. *It's got to be him.* He rushed to answer it.

Brandon stood in the hallway holding a bouquet of red and white carnations wrapped in green florist's paper. "Hi. I guess I'm in the right place." He wore faded blue jeans and a crisp, baby-blue shirt showed under his leather biker's jacket.

"Brandon, please come in. It's so good to see you! And you brought flowers!" He took them and inhaled their scent. "That's so sweet."

"Well, I thought I should bring something, but I didn't know what you were fixing for dinner. So I settled on flowers. I hope that's all right."

"It's wonderful. You didn't have to bring anything, but this was so nice of you." He ushered him in. "Let me take your jacket." He placed the flowers on the hall table before hanging the jacket in the tiny entry closet. Retrieving the bouquet, he said, "I'll put these in a vase, and we can use them for our table setting tonight. Come on, follow me."

Brandon trailed after him into the kitchen, his eyes wide. "This is a magnificent place, Rick. It's beautiful, and the view is marvelous."

"We like it." Rick fussed over the flowers. "I don't have dinner quite finished. You said you weren't allergic to seafood, right?"

"I love seafood. Is there anything I can do to help?"

"Well, I was just about to slice the fennel. If you don't mind, you could do that. Thin slices, as thin as you can."

Brandon looked at the ingredients on the counter. "Uh, which one's fennel?"

"Oh, sorry. It's that bulb with the feathery leaves. Chop off the stalk—we don't need it.

Then just slice it like an onion. Be careful, though, the knife is sharp."

"I can cook. I taught myself when I was with...I taught myself before." He sliced into the vegetable while Rick disappeared to place the flowers on the table. Brandon's voice drifted to him from the kitchen. "Hey, it smells kind of like licorice."

"Yeah, it's the plant that anise comes from." Rick came back and started slicing the green beans.

Brandon swore. "Ouch! Damn it! Now I've done it."

Rick whirled and saw Brandon sucking on a finger. "What's wrong? Let me see." He took his hand and examined the cut. "It's not bad, but we should put some ointment on it. Come along."

He led him to the bathroom, where he washed the wound and applied Bacitracin and a Band-Aid. "There. It'll be as good as new in no time."

Brandon grinned and reached to touch Rick's jaw. "I see you had a boo-boo, too." He held out the speck of tissue, now blotted and ruddy.

Rick felt his face heat. "I forgot about that. I shaved after my shower this afternoon and cut myself. Haven't done that in years. I must have looked like an idiot, with that stuck on me."

"You looked kind of cute, actually." Brandon shook his head and looked at his bandaged finger. "I'm such a klutz. I cut myself all the time when I was cooking for, you know, that other person. He used to say I'd cut my hand off someday and serve it to him."

"I'm sorry, but from what I've seen of Peter Warren, he'd eat your hand and think it was his God-given right."

Brandon grinned at that. "Yeah, he was pretty much a total jerk. I don't know why I stayed with him as long as I did."

"You deserve better, that's for sure." Silence nestled between them for a moment. "Well, what say I finish fixing dinner? Since you're the walking wounded, we'll have some wine and you can watch, how's that?"

"Well, there must be something I can do. Set the table, maybe?"

"It's all set, I'm afraid." Back in the kitchen, Rick pulled down a bottle of Riesling and handed Brandon a corkscrew. "How about you open the wine and pour us each a glass? The goblets are there on the counter. I'm almost done here anyway."

"Sure, I can do that."

Rick sliced tomato and onion and chopped them with the food processor. He finished slicing the fennel and mixed it together with the green beans, vinegar, and fresh basil in a large bowl. Finally, he tossed the lobster, scallops, crab, and shrimp in with the mixture.

"That really smells and looks wonderful."

"I thought we'd have something light. There's a market for tenants down on the forty-fourth floor that steamed and shelled the seafood for me. Oh, the salad's in the refrigerator. You want to get it out and put it on the table?"

"Okay." He opened the refrigerator, pulled out the crystal bowl, and removed the plastic wrap from the top. "This looks great. More seafood?"

"Yeah. I'll be interested in seeing what you think of it. Let's go." He carried his wine and the bowl with the main course to the dining table.

Brandon placed the salad on the table and stood before the window facing the North Shore. "This is incredible. It's like the stars all fell to earth and are laid out there for us to admire."

"It's a great view. The real estate agent told us we could see Michigan across the lake on a clear day, but I don't think we're high enough."

"You can see Michigan from the Observatory on the top floor. Or at least, they told us that on the tour." He placed a palm on the window and leaned his forehead against the glass. "I'd never get anything done if I had a view like this in my room."

Rick's heart warmed at the longing in Brandon's voice. "I guess I take it for granted, having lived here for so long."

"Mmm. I thought you said you had an estate in Wisconsin? Somehow I thought you lived there."

"Lindermont Manor. Yes, that's the Montgomery family estate. I guess that's where I officially live. That's where I vote, or at least cast my absentee ballot. It's in southwest Wisconsin, not terribly far from the Iowa border. But when I'm working at the bank, I live here."

"Well, it's beautiful." His blue eyes glittered as he turned back to Rick. "Thank you for showing me. Peter had a nice apartment, but nothing like this."

"Thanks. I did have some help decorating, and the view came with the condo." He pointed to the table. "Sit. We should eat before things get cold."

Rick watched while Brandon helped himself. He smiled as a look of surprise washed across Brandon's face at the first bite of the salad.

"Hey, this is great." Brandon's words sang with delight. "It tastes just like a California roll, except it's a salad. How clever!"

"Ah, so you've had sushi before?"

"Yeah. My first boyfriend was training to be a sushi chef. We ate his practice runs all the time. This is fantastic."

"I confess, I'm a bit disappointed. I'm used to people telling me they won't eat sushi, that it's bait. Then, when they like my salad, I inform them that they must like sushi after all, since they just ate some."

"Cute. The other thing is great too. I've never had anything with, what did you say it was called? The licorice thing?"

"Fennel. It's not always in season, but it adds a nice piquancy, don't you think?"

"Piquancy. Yes." Brandon's smile lit up the room and dazzled more than the view out the windows ever could. "Not many people would think to use that word."

"I always say, why use a monosyllable when polysyllabic elucidation will suffice?"

"That's a good one. My rhetoric teacher told me I used too many big words in my papers."

"He's an idiot. You can tell him I said so, and I'm a Regent for Montgomery College." He sipped his wine. "Tell me about your studies, Brandon."

"You know I have this dream of being a doctor someday. I can do the first two years of pre-med online, and I'm almost done with that. But the rest of it has a lot of lab work, and I'll have to do that in residence someplace. That's going to be hard, but I'll figure it out."

"I'm sure you will. I can tell you're bright, and determined too. That's a winning combination. You know, I don't do much as a Regent other than give them money, but I understood that most students nowadays get government grants and loans to finance their schooling. Have you checked into that?"

"Yeah. It'd help some for most of the costs, but it wouldn't quite cover living expenses."

"Your parents won't help?"

"My dad disappeared when I was two. I have no idea where he's at. And my mother...she kicked me out when I was sixteen. She found me making out with my boyfriend, and, well, that was that."

"Brandon! How did you live?"

"There's a shelter up in Boys Town that helps gay kids whose parents abuse them or kick them out of the house. I lived there until I graduated from high school. Social Services chipped in some too. It didn't hurt that I was a straight-A student. That's about the only thing that's ever been straight about me." He grinned.

"Well, you've done well for yourself. You should be proud."

After dinner, Rick gathered dishes from the table while Brandon rinsed them and loaded the dishwasher. It seemed to Rick that they worked in perfect harmony, as if they'd been doing this task together for years.

Brandon drained the water from the sink and wiped soap suds from his hands with a paper towel. "That was a wonderful meal. Thank you." He paused for a beat. "But I liked the companionship best of all. It's been a long time since I've felt that relaxed, that at home with someone." He put a hand over his mouth. "I'm sorry. That sounds pushy, like I'm flirting with you."

"If it was flirting, I liked it. I felt the same way. It's been lonely, staying here. Sandra, my sister-in-law, lives across the hall. We go out some, but this was different."

"I remember her. Did you know she and I had lunch together in Sedona? She's really nice. I had the feeling she, uh, thinks a lot of you."

"She and I went to school together." Rick hesitated, but decided against telling Brandon about his history with Sandra. "Shall we sit in the living room? I could put on some music, if you like?"

"That'd be nice."

"What would you like to listen to?"

"Anything. Well, not rap or techno. Anything else."

"I've got a CD of Michael Feinstein singing Gershwin show tunes. Is that too corny for you?"

"Hey, I love Feinstein. I have a bunch of his CDs. Or had. I guess Peter has them now."

"I'll make a deal with you. I won't talk about Victoria if you won't talk about Peter."

Brandon grinned. "That's a deal I can live with, for sure." He settled on the sofa. "Wow, I've never felt leather this soft. This is a pretty cool design, too, real modern."

"I like it, but it's kind of out of style. The interior decorator called it a 'sofa in a cage' because of the stainless steel framing."

Brandon laughed out loud at that. "That sure describes it. I still like it, and the chairs too."

Rick hesitated, trying to decide between the chair and the sofa. The ineluctable melody of "Someone to Watch Over Me" floated between them, the syllables lilting in Feinstein's mellifluous voice.

Brandon leaned back and gazed at him through hooded eyes. "Remember, when we were in Hidden Canyon, you said you were longing for someone to watch over you?"

"I remember. You said you were, too."

"And you held me. That was so wonderful. I needed that so much right then. That was when I knew I had to leave Peter, that there is more to life than he could ever give me."

Rick swallowed and wondered where this could be leading. "I remember holding you, and you holding me. I felt safe, somehow, with you in my arms. It felt right."

"Do you think...maybe...you might hold me again? Like that afternoon?" Brandon's voice was a whisper that warmed his heart.

Without a word, he settled on the sofa and put his arm about the younger man. Brandon snuggled into him, brushing his hair against Rick's throat and resting his head against his chest. "I can hear your heartbeat. I love the sound."

Rick didn't trust himself to speak. He inhaled Brandon's musky scent, and his lips brushed across the hairs on the other man's head. Sensations divine and glorious welled up inside him, and his hands trembled. Brandon's fingers teased at his torso and left a trail of golden pleasure behind them. He couldn't breathe, he couldn't think, he could only feel.

"Your heart is beating like thunder. I can hear it," Brandon murmured. "Listen. Can you hear it, too?"

"I can't help it." His words shuddered between them. "It's what you do to me, how you make me feel. It's all about you. It's been about you ever since I first saw you." He reached for Brandon's chin and tipped his face up. "God help me, I think I'm falling in love with you." His voice shook even as his body surged with yearning.

"That's incredible. I've thought the same thing ever since we watched that sunset together at Cathedral Rock. How I've longed to say it to you, and now it's done." His fingers ran through Rick's hair, and he pulled him close. "Kiss me, please, so I'll know this is real and not just a hopeless fantasy."

Rick let his lips graze Brandon's, inhaling the other's breath. Brandon's fingers, gentle and sublime, found their way inside his shirt where they swept over his skin and wound their way to his side, pulling him closer. Brandon pressed harder against him, his mouth open and his moist tongue slipping inside Rick's mouth. Their bodies and souls meshed and synchronized, hearts beating and breaths pulsing in unison. Rick dared to twine his tongue about Brandon's and then to probe his depths. At last, gasping, he had to break away.

"I didn't know it could be like this. You're so perfect, so sweet. Like we were made for each other." Rick let his fingers tease through Brandon's hair, luxuriating in the coarse, masculine feel. He let his cheek stroke against Brandon's beard, delighting in the raspy reminder that this was a man in his arms.

Brandon's fingers undid the top three buttons on Rick's shirt and he lowered his lips to his throat, where a moist fire blazed with every caress. The kisses traced lower, finding their way to his chest, then to his nipples.

"You taste so good, so manly," Brandon whispered. His hand brushed over Rick's left nipple, while his tongue danced a slow pirouette over the right one. "Tell me this was meant to be, that it will always be like this."

"How I've wanted to touch you, to hold you. I never imagined I could feel this way about anyone, ever. Yes, we're meant to be. I know that now. You have the keys to my heart, as no one ever could."

Brandon's voice shook with emotion. "Rick, the medallion I gave you." He stared at it, where it rested on Rick's chest. "You wore it for me, for tonight." Tears welled in his eyes, and he wiped at them. "When your heart's ablaze, I guess smoke gets in your eyes," he misquoted.

"I've worn it every day since you gave it to me, so I wouldn't forget you. To give me hope."

"Hope. Yes. I know that hope. I've always longed for someone to love me, to watch over me." He pulled away and stripped off his shirt. "I need to give myself to you, tonight, right now. I can't wait any longer."

Chapter Eight

"We've Only Just Begun"

His body quivering with desire, Brandon stooped to untie his sneakers. When he stood and kicked them off, a thrill passed through him as Rick's eyes ranged over his body. "Do you like the way I look?" His fingers traced a line from his chest to the snap on his blue jeans, following the treasure trail of hair that disappeared into his pants. Out of the corner of his eye he glimpsed the window and the constellation of city lights that glittered up the lake shore next to the still darkness of the waters. *Just like we're in heaven.*

The gleam in Rick's face outdid the stupendous view. "You're beautiful, did you know that? I love the way I can see your muscles flow underneath the hairs on your chest and stomach. It's like you have the same five o'clock shadow all over, just like your beard. It's revealing and masculine at the same time."

Brandon let a sly grin play with his features. "I'm glad you like it." He unsnapped his jeans and pulled the zipper halfway down. His cock, still confined in his jockey shorts and bound by the tight denim of his pants, ached to be free. "But I'd like to see more of you." He reached out to where Rick still lounged on the sofa and undid the rest of the buttons on the other's shirt. As the last came free, he untucked it and let it flutter open. Grasping him by both hands, he pulled Rick to his feet and slipped his fingers behind his back. "Come to me. I need my whole body to touch yours."

He closed his eyes and swirled his torso against Rick's, letting his fingers trace a fine line up from the other man's waist to his armpits. He pulled Rick's shirt back off his shoulders and buried his lips in his exposed neck, inhaling his man-scent. His fingers floated over Rick's chest and abdomen, thrilling at the hard ridges of muscle rippling under the other man's smooth skin.

Rick twisted out of his shirt and let it drop to the floor. His lips found their way to Brandon's ear, where his tongue played a melody of sensual delight before moving lower to his neck. His hands, strong and demanding, slipped inside Brandon's jeans, then underneath his shorts. "That feels so wonderful," he whispered, pulling Brandon's cock free and stroking it with gentle fingers.

Brandon gasped and gave his jeans an impatient tug, letting them fall to his ankles. He kicked out of them and jerked his shorts to his knees, where they fell to the floor. He pressed against Rick's body, luxuriating in the feel of his naked cock against Rick's crisp chinos and delighting in the hard rod that he found underneath them, straining against the fabric.

Rick's hands gripped his ass and pulled him closer. A whisper floated in his ear between moist kisses. "We should go to the bedroom, don't you think?"

"I'll follow you anywhere."

Rick pulled back and grinned. "I just might hold you to that." He took Brandon's hand and led him through a dark, paneled door to where a teak platform bed with a brown and black comforter dominated the room.

Brandon stared at the framed picture on the nightstand. "Rick, it's our picture from Sedona. By your bedside!" Brandon traced a finger on the snapshot that Eddie had taken of them months ago at Secret Canyon. "You know, that's where I keep my copy, too."

"I think Eddie must have sensed more about us that day than either of us knew or dreamed." Rick pulled the sheets back on the bed and slipped out of his pants and underwear.

Brandon's eyes widened as he at last took in his lover's full glory. "You look almost like a bodybuilder or a Greek statue by Praxiteles. Or an illustration of the male body in an anatomy book, you're so perfect." He let his gaze linger on what soared from Rick's crotch. "And you've got just about the most beautiful cock I've ever seen. If I'd known you were that...endowed...I wouldn't have let you get away so easily back in that canyon in Sedona."

"You're no slacker yourself in that department." Rick lay in the bed and patted the mattress next to him. "Come here, you."

Brandon hopped into the bed and kissed him on the lips. Aching to do more, to touch him more, he held back, knowing that the longer this took the more profound it would be for both of them. He moved lower, kissing Rick's chest, then his navel, and finally the dark bush between his legs. Rick's intoxicating scent drove him forward, and his tongue tasted the tip of his erection, sampling the clear fluid leaking from him. "You taste good, did you know that?"

Rick pulled Brandon's head away. "I'm an idiot. I don't have any condoms." His jaws tensed and his brow furrowed. "There's an all-night pharmacy a few blocks away."

Brandon tried not laugh, but didn't quite succeed. "I've got two in my pants back in the living room." He bounced out of bed and raced to the other room to retrieve them.

When he returned to the bedroom, Rick was still in bed, still hard and with a small smile playing over his features. "So did you know we were going to end up in bed tonight, or are you always this prepared?"

"I dreamed we might make love tonight, but I never dared to imagine we really would." Kneeling next to Rick on the bed, he tore open one of the packages with his teeth. "Remember, I told you I lived in that shelter for gay kids up on Halsted? They told us to always have condoms for safe sex. It's not like they encouraged us to sleep around—just the opposite. But they drilled us about being prepared and not taking risks. So, I always have a couple with me, from habit." He paused and looked around. "Uh, you don't have any lube, do you?"

"Sorry, no."

"It's okay. These come with some lube already. Hold still." He pulled back on Rick's erection and slipped the latex on with a slow, slithering motion. "Sorry it's red. It's cherry flavored."

"That's fine. Let me put yours on you."

"Let's save it. I want you inside me, fucking me, first. I won't need one for that." He plopped onto his back and put a pillow under his hips. "Come here, you hot man. I need our bodies to touch, to have my legs and arms wrap around you and to have you inside me."

Brandon spread his legs, and Rick knelt between them. With one hand Rick stroked his cock, and with the other he touched Brandon's, his eyes wide. "It's like a miracle," he breathed. "You're so beautiful, and here you are, with me, attracted to me." He leaned down, and his hot breath wafted across Brandon's cock and balls. Brandon gasped as Rick took first one, then the other of the round spheres in his mouth. His mouth traversed backward, then kissed him behind where they hung. After that, he moved higher, and his kisses found Brandon's steely rod, climbing up the shaft to the crown.

Brandon shuddered when a sudden, warm moistness engulfed him. "God, that's nice, but don't do that yet. Come here and kiss my lips." He pulled Rick's head up and wrapped his arms about him, pulling him close and stroking his back. "You feel so good against me." He wrapped his legs around Rick's and pulled him closer. "Are you ready? I want you so bad!"

"Me, too. I had no idea it could be like this...."

Brandon rested his ankles on Rick's shoulders and let some saliva pool in his palm. He grinned. "It's a natural lubricant. I'll guide you in." His head lolled back and he gripped that rigid hose that grew from Rick's loins. His body trembled with his need as their hard cocks touched. He guided Rick's dick back, behind his balls, where it brushed against his scrotum, then yet further back. "There, oh God, yes." He relaxed his sphincters as Rick entered him.

Rick's body hovered over him, his eyes closed, his chest touching Brandon's thighs. As if playing a delicate Mozart adagio, he pressed deeper, receded, then inserted himself deeper yet, in a slow, gentle rhythm. Their bodies, locked together at last, rocked in an accelerating melody of mutual bliss. Not too fast, not too slow, Rick's thrusts sang a perfect duet with Brandon's needs. Their bodies grew slick with perspiration that pooled on Brandon's chest in a glorious blending of their mutual desire.

Their bodies danced ever faster, their heartbeats drummed in a thunderous cadence, and their souls sang the ancient harmonies of two spirits conjoined as one. Their pairing electrified Brandon's body in ways he'd never felt before. Rick's cock thrust deep inside, almost departed, and then came back once more, threatening to split him in half even as it joined the two of them together. Above him Rick's face contorted and his muscles tensed as he called out, thrust forward, and ground into him. A groan rasped in Brandon's throat and escaped his clenched teeth. For an instant, for an eternity, his mind dissolved while his body seized him in a paroxysm of ecstasy. His arms reached out and pulled Rick closer, his hips rolled to pull him deeper, and his muscles gripped at his thrusting cock, yearning for deliverance. Hot fluids jetted forth from him and splattered, first on his chest, then higher on his lips and his forehead.

Too soon, his mind regained control of his physical being. Rick rested over him, on his palms. Sweat beaded on his forehead and a trickle dripped from the tip of his nose. He heaved a huge breath and flopped onto his back. His voice shook. "I never imagined it could be like that."

"You were incredible. It was the best I've ever had, too." Brandon's fingers wiped the cum from his face, astounded at the power of his orgasm.

"No, you don't understand." Little sobs escaped Rick's throat. "It was beautiful, so beautiful. All my life sex has been this mechanical thing, something to do that feels good. Like a fine wine, or a good meal. But with you, tonight, it was so different! You've changed my life." He wiped tears from his cheeks. "You must think I'm an idiot."

Brandon blinked back the tears welling in his own eyes, and then decided to let them flow. "It was beautiful, wasn't it? Almost like a religious experience."

"That's it exactly. There, between the two of us, I know I sensed something divine. It was you and me, and the universe, all together, dancing the most perfect ballet ever. My heart sang to music I'd never heard before, never imagined existed." He shook his head and cuddled closer. "I can't describe it. It's like I've lived my whole life only half-alive, and now, because of you, the blinders have fallen from my eyes and I can see the world as it really is. And it's beautiful."

"Life is beautiful. You're beautiful." Brandon's fingers combed through Rick's hair, while his heart ached to make this wonderful man happy. "We'll have to do it again." Laughter bubbled up from his throat. "I hear it gets better with practice."

"That's hard to imagine. Much better than that, and I'll die from heart failure." Rick rose to an elbow and ran a finger over the milky fluids clinging to Brandon's chest hair. "I should get a towel for you." He looked down at where the condom had slipped free and rested in his own thatch. "For me, too." He sniffed and wiped his nose. "I'm a mess."

Brandon followed him into the bathroom and inspected the shower. "This thing has nozzles all over the place. It looks big enough for two. You want to try it?"

"Sure. Let me program it for a cold needle shower, followed by a gentle rinse."

Brandon shivered as the cold water drummed against his skin, then relaxed into the warm drizzle that followed. He rubbed soap onto one of the heavy washcloths and bathed Rick's body. "I love the way you feel."

"We're a pair, all right. One smooth, one hairy, one old, one young...."

"You're not old." Brandon ran soapy fingers over Rick's cock, and it hardened in response. "See. Aren't you glad we saved that other condom?"

* * * *

Brandon woke to the odors of bacon frying and coffee brewing. He stretched and glanced around the bedroom. His gaze lingered on the dent in the pillow where Rick had slept, and a smile turned his lips upward. He leaned forward and inhaled his scent. *It really happened.*

He sat up and cupped his palm over his mouth. *Ugh. Morning breath.* Someone, no doubt Rick, had left a white terrycloth robe draped over the foot of the bed. He picked it up, and the weight of the plush fabric dragged at his fingers. Wrapping it around him, he retreated to the bathroom in search of a toothbrush.

"I see you're awake."

He turned to see Rick standing in the doorway, wearing an identical robe. "Yeah. I borrowed a toothbrush. I hope that's all right."

"I think I can spare one. I let you sleep. I hope you didn't need to get up this morning."

"I don't work today. They moved me to the weekend, so Thursday's my day off."

"Good. I was thinking we might do something together today. I called the bank and told them I wouldn't be in."

Brandon leered at him. "Just what did you have in mind doing?"

Rick dimpled. "Well, I had that in mind, too. But I thought we'd go out. There's a new exhibit at the Field Museum, and there's a string quartet recital at the Chicago Conservatory. They're doing Bartok."

"Never heard of him. But if you like him, I'm sure I will, too."

"Tonight, I thought we'd go out for dinner, someplace nice, before coming back here." He blushed. "Look at me. I'm assuming you're going to spend tonight here too. You've probably got boyfriends coming out of your ears."

Brandon dug a finger in one ear, and then opened his robe and looked himself over. "No boyfriends coming from any orifice, so far as I can tell." He looked back at Rick, whose eyes were twinkling. "Except for the one standing right next to me. Just try and keep me from spending the night. If you'll have me."

"Always and forever. Oh, and we need to shop, too."

"Groceries? How domestic! I love it!"

"Uh, I was thinking of certain purchases at a drugstore...."

"Oh. Well, that's kind of domestic, too, in its own way."

"I guess that's true. Look, flirting is fun, but breakfast is getting cold. The Trib should be here by now. You want to get it from the hallway while I dish things up in the kitchen?"

Brandon strode through the condo to the front entry. The living room looked completely different in the daylight, dazzling white walls over the dark flooring and black leather furniture. White puffballs of clouds drifted over the clear blue of the lake. "Looks like it's going to be a great day," he called out.

He opened the front door and stooped to pick up the paper. The tenant across the hall chose that moment to step out of her apartment. Brandon fixed a smile on his face and stood to greet her.

"Brandon?" Sandra clutched at her designer, camel-colored coat and stared at him.

"Ms. Montgomery!" Panic snatched his breath away. Rick had told him she lived across the hall, and he'd forgotten. *Oh God, I've really screwed the pooch now. What do I say to her?*

Sandra's eyes widened as she looked him over, taking in his robe and the open apartment door behind him. "Brandon, *darling!*" She laughed, and her smile twinkled at him. "Rick's found someone *nice,* at last." She put both hands on his shoulders and pecked him on the cheek. "I couldn't be happier for both of you. I guess this makes us in-laws. Or in-laws squared. Or something." She walked a few steps down the hall to the elevator and pushed the down button. "Don't tell that old fuddy-duddy I saw you, or at least don't tell him until I'm there to see his face." She winked at him as the elevator dinged and the doors opened. Still chuckling, she disappeared.

Chapter Nine

"The Long and Winding Road"
Christmas Eve 2008

Rick dumped the last box from Brandon's room into the back of his SUV and inspected the cargo. Four battered cardboard cartons, two of which contained nothing but books, filled the rear cargo space. A laundry bag stuffed with linens and underwear, and a couple dozen shirts on hangers rested on top of the boxes. *Poor kid, that's everything he owns in the world.* A momentary pang of guilt pulsed through Rick as he glanced at the two Louis Vuitton satchels—gifts from Victoria—that held the few things he needed for the trek to Lindermont Manor. He slammed the hatch shut, shivered in the frigid wind from the lake, and turned to his companion. "You ready?"

Brandon's breath puffed from his mouth and flew away in the morning gusts. "Yeah." He looked over the run-down tenement where he'd been living. "I won't miss this place, that's for sure." His hair fluttered about his head, and his cheeks were pink flames in the chill morning air. An amber halo clung about the globes of the streetlights overhead, and an orange glow from the rising sun had just begun to tinge the eastern sky.

"Hop in. It's friggin' *cold* out here this morning." Rick slid into the passenger seat, while Brandon climbed in on the driver's side and started the engine.

Rick rubbed his gloved hands over his arms. "Thank God for heated seats." He glanced at the car's console. "It's four below."

"But it's nice and warm in here." Brandon ran his hands over the heated leather. "I love these seats. How far is it to Lindermont?"

"If the roads hold up, it'll take two or three hours at most. Get on I-90, and we'll take it to Rockford."

Brandon eased out from the curb, and the tires crunched on the dusting of snow that had fallen in the night. "I can find the interstate without any help. I'll need directions when we get off, though."

"We'll swap when we stop for breakfast and I'll drive the rest of the way, if you like. There's a place in Rockford there with great down-home cooking. After that, we'll take Highway 20 for about sixty miles. Then it's kind of hit or miss on state and county routes to Lindermont."

"At least there's not much traffic this morning." He passed through a cloud of diesel fumes from a CTA bus and pulled up to a stoplight.

"Yeah. Leaving this early, we'll miss most of the people traveling on Christmas Eve. I'm sorry I cut it so short, but there were last-minute things at the bank I couldn't put off."

"That's all right. What with the scholarship, I could afford to quit my job last week at Nike Town, and I liked having some time off. I used it to finish up the last of my online courses, so now I'll be ready to focus on classes in the spring semester at Montgomery

College." He patted Rick's hand. "Thanks for getting me in there."

"I had nothing to do with it. You deserved it, and the scholarship you got, too. Sandra's on the committee, and she would have thrown things your way if she had to, but she said you were at the top of the list. Hey, let's stop at that Donutland and pick up some coffee."

"Well, I'm still grateful to you both." Brandon wheeled the vehicle into the almost empty parking lot. "I looked up the chair of the Biology program at Montgomery, Dr. LeClerc. He's really well-known."

"Doesn't he study dogs, or something like that?"

"He's an experimental geneticist specializing in the canine genome. He's got a bunch of grants."

"Yeah, the Board's always approving purchase orders for gene sequencers for him. I've met him; he's nice. His spouse is chief of security for the campus."

"A female chief of security? That's cool."

"No, a gay chief of security. That's even cooler. Sondergard's also undersheriff for the county, so he's got arrest authority on campus. He solved some big serial killer case back when he and LeClerc were both students in Oregon. We're lucky to have them at our little college. I'll get the coffee, you keep the car warm. You do want some, right?"

"Can't live without it."

The snow crunched under their feet as they left the restaurant in Rockford. Rick raised his eyebrows at Brandon when they approached their car. "You want me to drive the rest of the way?"

"If you don't mind? I just need to sit back and digest after that breakfast. I'm not used to eating that much in the morning."

"But it was good, wasn't it?"

"You bet. The Denver omelet alone was more than I usually eat all day."

Rick drove through the city streets and observed, "Well, the traffic's still not bad."

"It's the economy. No one's spending as much or traveling as much as they did last year."

"From what I've read, it's the worst holiday for retailers since the seventies."

"My boss told me sales were down in our department at Nike Town. I don't think they missed me when I quit."

Rick nodded. "I'm glad we were so cautious at the bank. Victoria, I mean some of the Board members, wanted us to buy into hedge funds and other things, but we stuck with safer, lower-return investments. Sorry, I'm boring you."

"Nothing about you bores me." He rubbed at the fog on his window. "This is sure flat, with nothing but endless corn fields. Where are the trees?"

"The corporate farms cultivate right up to the fence rows. They've cut down most of the trees. It'll look different when we get to the hills around Lindermont. We've still got old-growth forest, with rolling hills and limestone bluffs along the river. I think you'll like it."

"You haven't told me much about the place. I take it that it's a big house?"

Rick snorted. "It's obscene. Victoria's grandparents built it back before the First World War. The name is an amalgam of her grandmother's maiden name, Linderman, and her married name, Montgomery. The original mansion had two immense wings, almost identical. One was for her grandparents. The other wing was big enough for another family to live in. The plan was that, when their newborn son grew up and married, he'd move into that wing and there'd be two happy families under one roof. From what I understand, the real goal was so Silas Montgomery could keep his son under his thumb."

"Nice. Just what the son wanted, I bet."

"Well, it worked. But Phineas was pretty much a controlling SOB himself after his father passed. He bought that condo for us in the John Hancock building because he already owned one on the floor above. That way he could keep an eye on us. He even added a third wing to Lindermont so that Sandra could move in with her future husband."

Brandon laughed. "That didn't work out according to plan, did it?"

"You mean because she never married?"

"Well, that. Plus, I can't see her knuckling under to anyone. I really like her." Rick nodded. "She's special. Given the way things worked out, with you and me I mean. I'm glad I didn't marry her. She held me together after Victoria disappeared. She's a rock."

"She told me all she wants is for us to be happy. She's sweet." Brandon smiled. "I'm glad she's going to spend Christmas with us."

"Me, too. I'm looking forward to a quiet dinner tonight. It's supposed to warm up tomorrow, so maybe we can walk the grounds."

"So it'll be just the three of us? Somehow I thought the place might be crawling with servants. You know, like in *Howard's End*."

Rick chuckled. "That's exactly what it used to be like, when old Phineas lived there. What a pretentious ass. We moved most of the servants to other jobs at the college or in the village after Victoria's parents moved out. Now we use the same maid service as the Holiday Inn in town, and there's a crew of Mexicans that take care of the gardens. There're only three permanent staff left in the Manor. Daniels manages the place for us, including the contract labor. Emma cooks and buys the groceries. And then there's James. He helped raise Victoria and Sandra, and we didn't have the heart to move him out. He's more or less retired, but we let him help, like old times, for his self-respect."

"Mr. Daniels, Emma, and James. I think I can keep track of three people. That's a relief."

"Don't worry about it. Daniels can be prickly, but the other two are just nice folks. Anyway, the staff should have Christmas Eve and Christmas Day off. James might be around, but we should be pretty much on our own."

Rick relaxed behind the wheel and let the miles speed by. The landscape grew more rugged, and trees sprang up here and there. When they pulled off Highway 20, the road snaked through low hills and scattered deciduous wildwood. Snow piled high on the shoulders, but the surface was clear. The SUV splashed through puddles of melted ice on the uneven blacktop, and Rick slowed even more. "When you drive to classes, you'll have to watch these roads. The puddles freeze overnight, and you can't see them. Black ice, the locals call it."

"How far is the campus from Lindermont?"

"About twenty miles. In good weather you can easily do it in thirty minutes, door to door. In ice and snow, it can take forever." He nodded to the front. "Lindermont Village is just ahead."

"There's a village named for where you live? Wow."

"Old Silas Montgomery ran the estate like a commercial operation. There was logging and farming, all done by hired hands. The village grew up to support them. Later, Phineas deeded most of the land to the county or the state for parks. Well, it was really for the tax deduction, but now most of the land around here is a wildlife preserve."

"It's charming." Brandon peered at the quaint buildings that clung to the hillside. "This is almost like a Swiss village in the middle of Wisconsin."

"More like the middle of nowhere. Dubuque's the biggest city around, about thirty miles from here and across the river in Iowa. And it's not much, trust me."

"I've lived in Chicago all my life. This will be a nice change."

"Tell me that in February, when we're snowed in and it's thirty below outside."

Brandon dimpled. "I'll just have to find some way to amuse you."

The SUV left the village, and Rick turned into a lane that led under a stone archway. "This is the entrance." A wrought iron gate, like the door to a cage but with spearpoints at the top of the bars, stood open. Just outside the gate, a sign read *Lindermont Manor, Private Property. Vendors please use the north entrance.*

A map underneath showed a circuitous route in red. The road ahead followed a gentle curve through a dense forest of barren trees, with a smattering of evergreens mixed in. Brown undergrowth protruded from the snow clinging to the surface. Dirty white lumps lay piled along the shoulders from where someone had plowed the road.

Rick sighed. "Not far now. This is really lovely in the fall, when the leaves change color."

"This is a private drive?"

"Yeah. Usually the gate's closed." He pointed to the buttons embedded in the SUV's rearview mirror. "The middle one opens the gate we just came through. The one on the far right opens the garage up at the house. You already know the one on the far left is for the parking garage in Chicago."

"I can't wait to see Lindermont Manor. It must be marvelous."

Rick pulled out his cell phone. "Marvelous isn't exactly the word I'd use. Let me call Sandra and let her know we're almost there. She should be here, unless she couldn't stand it and already fled to Dubuque." He snorted, muttered into the phone, and flipped it shut. "She's there, and they'll be watching for us. It won't be long now."

Brandon waved at the snow-encrusted underbrush and limestone outcrops. "This is nice now, but I bet it's fantastic when things turn green."

"Yeah. There's a big tradition every spring when the tulips and hyacinths bloom. We open up the grounds and let the locals in to enjoy the flowers." At a Y-junction in the road, he turned left and pointed to the right. "That way leads to the old carriage house, from the horse-and-buggy days."

The SUV wound its way to the top of a hill and slowed to a stop. On the other side of a small valley, Lindermont Manor soared on the brow of a gentle hill. Rick remained quiet and watched Brandon's reaction. In front of them, a lawn adorned with evergreen shrubs rose to an immense Tudor-style mansion. Pathways marked by rough stone fences coiled through the snow. Two immense, identical wings thrust forward from the central core of the mansion itself. A round tower stood above the entryway and ended in a pointed, conical roof. Shake shingles covered everything, and dormers sprang from the roofs in perfect, symmetrical rows. The drive curved up the hill and circled around an ice-covered pond before looping back to rejoin itself. A spur ran off to one side, where a smaller, Tudor-style structure served as a garage.

Rick's lips turned up, and he nodded to the main entrance. "When we get to the door, let Daniels unload our things and put the car away."

"Okay. I can help."

"It's what we pay him to do. Hey, there's Sandra!" He pointed to a distant figure waving from the covered entry. Another figure emerged from the double doors and handed her a coat.

Rick drove the rest of the way to the Manor. He smiled at Brandon, noting that his eyes were wide with wonder, or maybe it was fear. Rick felt a pang of guilt for not preparing him better for this place. He remembered how intimidating it was the first time he'd visited. "Don't worry. They're nice people. Daniels is okay, really. His mother worked for Victoria's parents and grandparents, so he's second generation." When they pulled up to the door, he hopped out. "Come on!" He ran up to Sandra and gave her a hug.

Sandra beamed at them. "Rick, it's so good to see you. And you, too, Brandon. You come here and give me a hug!"

"Hi, Sandra. I'm glad to see you're here." He embraced her and stood back. "This is, uh, different than what I expected."

An older man who had been hovering behind Sandra walked to the car and opened the front door. "Oh, excuse me, sir?" He raised his eyebrows at Rick. "You wouldn't have the car keys, would you, sir?"

Brandon fished in his pocket. "Here, take mine."

Before he could move, the old fellow was at his side and accepted them with a slight bow. "Thank you, sir."

Sandra smiled. "Brandon, this is James. He'll unload your things and put the car away. He all but raised me. He taught me to tie my shoes when I was little."

Brandon held out his hand. "James, it's so nice to meet you."

He looked surprised. "Why, yes, sir. And you, too." His voiced husked in the cold, and he rushed to open the rear hatch.

Rick called out, "James, take the boxes to the Green Suite. Brandon will be staying there. My bags are in the back, and they go in the Blue." He turned to Sandra. "Where are you staying? In your wing?"

"God, no. It's so dreary. No one's been there for at least two years since people stayed there for that thing we had for the bank. If you don't mind, I'll stay in Daddy's old rooms, in the West Wing." She leaned into him and whispered. "Then the two of you can have some privacy. Just don't scream and shout when you do it, okay? I don't think James' heart could take it."

He frowned at her and whispered back, "Shh, now. You'll scandalize the nice old fellow." His voice rose. "Where's Daniels, anyway? The front gate was open."

"Daniels! I swear, I'm going to strangle that man yet. I'm so sorry, Rick, I know you wanted a quiet Christmas Eve."

"So what's to stop us? It's just the three of us, right? The staff should have the holiday off."

"Wrong. The furnace in the village church went out, and Daniels told the Vicar he could have midnight mass here. The choir's coming this afternoon to practice. I'm so mad at Daniels I could spit. He didn't ask or anything, he just did it."

"Shit! There'll be a hundred people here, at least. We'll have to put up decorations and have food out. He damned well should have asked first."

"That's what I told him. You know what he's like. He was all 'yes, Miss Cassandra' and 'no, Miss Cassandra.' But he damned well does what he pleases. Anyway, it's too late now. At least he's taken care of all the arrangements. I had James put a small tree in your rooms so the two of you can have a private celebration if you want."

"I'll still have to go the mass. That damned Vicar will have a fit if I don't go to services in my own home." He turned to Brandon and sighed. "I'm so sorry. I had no idea...."

"Hey, it's okay. It could even be fun. Uh, what kind of church is it?"

"It's sort of an independent church. You don't have to go if you don't want to. They use the Anglican book of prayer, but they're not part of the denomination. They were Episcopal once, but Silas got mad at the national denomination over ordaining women priests and the local congregation broke away."

Brandon gave him a determined look. "I want to go. I'm looking forward to it. Christmas eve mass right here in your own home. How cool is that?"

"At least it'll be in the Great Hall, which is kind of separate from the family quarters where we'll be staying."

Brandon shivered. "Can we go inside? I want to see, but it looks like I'll need a ball of string to find my way around. Unless you've got maps?"

Sandra hooked her arm through Brandon's. "Let me give you the grand tour. Rick, you go chew out that asshol Daniels."

Rick sighed, not looking forward to a confrontation. "Now, Sandra. It's Christmas, after all. I'll dress him down some other time, just for you, okay?"

"Well, it'd be a good Christmas present to me if you just fired his sorry...I mean, if you let him go. But I know we can't do that. Let me give Brandon the tour of my childhood home instead. You run along and unpack."

Chapter Ten

"Back Home Again"

Brandon blinked against the relative gloom of the mansion's interior after the bright, mid-day light outdoors.

Sandra tugged at his arm. "Come on. We'll get the Great Hall out of the way first, and then I'll show you to your rooms." She paused and grinned at him. "Sorry. Momma always said the first thing to show your guest was the where the restrooms are located. They're right here, off the cloakroom."

James shuffled through the door after them, carrying two of Brandon's boxes stacked one atop the other. He stooped to place them on the floor, treating them as if they held the most delicate of crystal. "Here, sir, let me take your coat."

Brandon let him slip the coat from his shoulders, feeling strange to have someone do this for him. "Thank you, James." He turned to Sandra. "I could stand a pit stop, if that's all right?" He shut himself into the lavish, marble-appointed room adjoining the entryway. *Jeez. This is almost as big as my bedroom back at Mom's place.* He took in the fresh flowers, the little spheres of scented soap, and the plush towels. *What have I gotten myself into?*

James, his coat, and the boxes had disappeared by the time he returned to the slate-floored entry. Two staircases swept in graceful curves on each side of the round room, rising to a marble balcony that overlooked the foyer. The ceiling soared higher yet, supporting a massive crystal chandelier. Wide hallways led to the left and right underneath the balcony, while broad stairs led down two steps into an immense room.

Sandra gripped his hand and pulled him forward. "This is the Great Hall. Back in the twenties, my grandparents had formal parties here almost every month."

The place bustled with at least fifty people hanging holiday decorations and setting up folding chairs, yet it seemed nearly empty to Brandon's eyes. Three fireplaces, with hearths so large he could walk into them without stooping, lined the walls on the left and the right, while a stage surmounted by an intricate stained glass window dominated the far end of the chamber. The ceiling vaulted above their heads in an intricate maze of timbers and joists, while the sun cast a rainbow of colors across the dark oak paneling. A circle of terrazzo laid in a compass-point pattern dominated the floor in the center of the room.

His breath caught in his throat. "This place is huge. How many people can you fit in here?"

A man with a scowl on his face and a clipboard in one fist scuttled up to them. "We'll set up for two hundred for services tonight, but we can put five hundred people in here if we need to." His tight tenor and precise enunciation matched his lean, wolf-like body. He faced Sandra, and his face twisted into what Brandon assumed must serve him for a smile. "Everything is under control, Miss

Cassandra, not to worry. We won't let Mrs. Collier's reputation for perfection diminish in her absence."

Her lips turned down. "I'm sure you won't. Brandon, this is Daniels. He's the estate manager. If you need anything at all, just let him know."

Daniels' eyes narrowed as his gaze ranged over Brandon from head to toe. "Ah, yes. You'll be Mr. Collier's house guest." He didn't extend his hand. "Did you bring any personal assistants with you, sir, or will the household staff be providing for your needs?"

"James can give him whatever help he needs, Daniels. See to it." Sandra's eyes snapped even though her voice stayed mild.

"Certainly, Miss Cassandra." He put the slightest emphasis on the "Miss," just enough to be noticed but not so much that anyone could object. "Mrs. Collier's standing orders are to take care of the guests of the Manor. Will Master Brandon be staying in the Guest House or in the Manor proper?"

"Mr. Collier gave directions for Brandon's things to be taken to the Green Suite in the East Wing. Mr. Collier will take the Blue, as usual."

"Ah, yes, adjoining rooms. I'll inform James." His face held no expression, but his voice seeped between them like cold maple syrup.

"James met us at the door. He already knows." Her eyes flitted around the disarray in the room. "This will all be ready for tonight?"

"Yes, ma'am. Oh, there's the piano tuner." He offered a curt bow. "If you will excuse me, Miss Cassandra. Sir." Without waiting for an answer, he raced away.

"Well, he seems to be quite efficient." Brandon stared at the retreating back while thinking that the man's manner reminded him of the way Sammy, his former boss at Nike Town, treated customers.

"That's not the word I'd use." Sandra didn't quite sneer. "Victoria let him get by with way too much, for hired help." She turned her attention back to Brandon. "The staff are good people, but some of them will run your life if you let them."

"Yeah, I know the type. Like a shoe salesman who wants to sell you those running shoes with Velcro when you want ones with laces."

She chuckled. "Exactly. They're hired to help you, not the other way around." She gave the Great Hall one last quick survey and took a deep breath. "Well, shall we take a look at your rooms?"

"Sure. Will I need a GPS receiver to find my way back here?"

"It's big, but you really can't get lost. The house is built like a fort, four wings surrounding the central courtyard that holds the Great Hall. There's one long hallway that runs all the way around, so if you just keep walking, you'll circumnavigate the whole place and wind up back where you started."

"Like Magellan. You know what happened to him."

"He sailed around the world, right?"

"Not quite. He died halfway there. The natives on some Pacific island killed him."

She smiled at that. "Well, the natives here are friendly. Or at least not deadly. I'm dying to see what you think of your rooms. Come on!"

She led him back to the entry and up one of the marble staircases. At the top, she pointed to the left. "That wing is where I grew up. Rick and Victoria moved into the East Wing, where Grandmama and Grandpapa lived when they were alive. After Daddy passed away, Momma moved to Sun City and Victoria took her old rooms. Rick liked the east wing better, though, so he kept his suite. The north wing, opposite where we are now, was where I was supposed to live."

"But you never did?"

"God, no. Sucking up to Daddy and surrounded by servants? That's for Victoria, not for me." She strode down the right-hand corridor, but Brandon held back.

"Hey, is that a dog I see?"

She turned and peered through the gloom in the opposing corridor. "Oh yes, that's Jasper. He is, or was, Victoria's dog."

"He's beautiful. What is he, a cocker spaniel? His fur looks like it's bright red."

"He's a cocker spaniel, and a purebred, of course. Victoria wouldn't tolerate anything else. His sire was a Grand Champion at the Westminster Dog Show. He's friendly enough, but he seems to miss Victoria. At least, he sleeps outside her door. Come on, the more interesting part of the house, where you'll be staying, is this way."

He followed after her, marveling at the interior appointments. Mahogany wainscoting and crisp, white plaster walls contrasted with the elegant sepia and salmon-colored Persian rugs that covered the marble flooring. Crystal chandeliers dangled at regular intervals over their heads, and the scent of fresh flowers wafted from the vases nestled in nooks in the walls. "This reminds me more of a fancy hotel than a home. The carpet, the paneling, the flowers; it's like the Drake back in Chicago."

"Victoria used some expensive interior designer when she redid the place after Momma moved out. It could be the same firm that did the Drake. Except that the artworks here are all original oils."

He paused in front of a sequence of paintings. "Who are these people?"

"That old man with the snarl on his face and the muttonchops is my grandfather. And the fat woman in the next painting, with that lovely smile? That's my grandmother. She always had that smile right before she smacked you for doing something that offended her."

"I'm sorry. They really hit you?"

"You mean that there are families that don't hit their children? My, what a novel idea that is!" She pointed to the next painting, the largest of them all. "That's my father."

"He looks serious, almost grim."

She ignored the comment and moved on to the next, and smallest, portrait, done in the impressionist style. "Here's Momma," she murmured.

"I love this one. She looks kind, but sort of sad, somehow."

"Brandon, dear, you're a genius at reading portraits, did you know that?"

"I guess I just see what the artist painted." He turned to gaze at another portrait, almost as large as the one of Sandra's father, which hung on the opposite side of the hallway.

"Who's this beauty? She looks like Vivian Leigh getting ready to meet Clark Gable in *Gone with the Wind*."

Sandra sniffed. "*That* is my sister, Victoria. She's always had a flair for the dramatic."

"She's really gorgeous." He turned to his companion and let his lips turn up. "I see the family resemblance."

"God, I hope not! Besides, she had a perfect figure, that raven-black hair and, well, look at me. If they had a picture next to the word mousy in the dictionary, it would be mine. Victoria, though, always had all kinds of men sniffing around her."

"Really, Sandra, you're beautiful. Your hair is golden brown with little flames of red hidden inside."

"You're a dear, but that's my hairdresser at work."

He looked around the hallway, but found no more portraits. "So, there's one of your sister. Where's yours?"

"I wouldn't let them do one of those dreadful things of me. Besides, I never earned mine." She nodded to Victoria's image. "This one was Daddy's reward for snagging an approved husband. Enough of this. Your room has some nice prints and no ghoulish ancestral paintings."

She led him around a corner and almost to the end of an interminable hallway, where she opened a set of double doors. "Here you are, the Green Suite."

He walked into a sitting room where a fire blazed in the hearth. Wallpaper with a light green filigree pattern over an ivory background adorned the walls, while the carpet was an emerald-colored Berber. A mahogany Queen Anne settee and chairs stood in front of the fireplace, and double glass doors led to the adjoining bedroom. French doors opened onto a small balcony over the central courtyard. The rooms were far enough north that he could see around the Great Hall to the west wing of the mansion.

"This is where I'll be staying?" Brandon felt his eyes widen.

"This is it." She pointed across the courtyard. "The windows on the far side, in the West Wing, are Momma's old rooms, the ones Victoria took over. I'll be staying on opposite side of the hall from those, in Daddy's old suite." She turned away from the window. "You can use the phone as an intercom. During the day, if you dial 0, you'll get Emma in the kitchen, if you need a snack or anything. There's a directory in the drawer for the other numbers. I'll be in the Phineas Suite, named for my Grandpapa. Oh, and that door over there?" She nodded toward the fireplace. "That goes to Rick's rooms. Convenient, huh?" She grinned at him, and Brandon's face heated with embarrassment.

"The bath adjoins the bedroom, and there's plenty of storage space." She opened a door into a cavernous closet. "I see that James left your things in here. Would you like to rest for a bit, or would you like more tour?"

He eyed the boxes. "I'm not looking forward to unpacking those boxes. And there's no bookcases in here. Can we maybe get some from someplace?"

"Hmm. Why don't you put your books in the Writing Room on the first floor? Victoria used it as her office, when she and Daniels planned parties here at the Manor. It's got a desk and the bookcases are mostly empty, plus no one is using it now."

"I don't think I should use the same room as Mrs. Collier. What will people think?"

"Who cares what people think? It's the perfect room for you to set up as your personal study. Go for it."

"What if Mrs. Collier comes back? Daniels made it sound like she'd just stepped out for coffee and would be back any time now." Brandon let his doubt show in his voice.

"He *wishes* she'd come back here, with what she let him get by with. It was like he was on a power high before she left." She sighed. "But I don't think she's ever going to return, Brandon. Rick wanted to avoid a scandal, and those fuddy-duddies at the bank hate negative publicity, so we told everyone that she's in Europe studying painting. She was always interested in art, and had even started to remodel the old carriage house as a studio. We encouraged the staff to think that her return is imminent."

"They believe that? And why wasn't there an investigation when she left? Rick won't talk to me about this at all."

"The staff believe what we tell them. There's no one to complain to the authorities except Rick and me, and we didn't, so there was no official investigation. We did ask the undersheriff to do some quiet checking. We knew she moved some money, actually a lot of money, out of the bank. The trail kind of vanishes in the Cayman Islands, and we couldn't trace it further without involving the

FBI, so we dropped it. Personally, I think she ran off with one of her lovers, but I'd never tell Rick that. In any case, for his sake and for the bank, we decided to pretend that this is an amicable separation."

"I don't get it. If she wanted to leave him, why not just divorce him?"

"Who knows why my sister does anything? I can see why Rick, the poor dear, wants to avoid the public humiliation of everyone knowing about her sleeping around with every Tom, Dick and Harry. As to Victoria, her pre-nup with Rick would have given him millions in a divorce settlement. My guess is that she just took her share of our inheritance and disappeared with it to screw him over."

"When she disappeared it must have been hard on Rick." He took her hand. "You, too. She's your sister."

"I'll live. And in my opinion, Rick's better off without her, even with the financial loss." She pulled away and turned toward the sitting room. "I could use a drink. There's a bar in the other room. Would you like something? Sherry, maybe?"

"No, thanks." He followed her out of the bedroom and watched her pour a brown fluid from a crystal carafe into a small goblet.

A discreet knock rapped at the door, and Brandon turned to see Daniels striding into the room. "Ahem, Miss Cassandra, may I interrupt you for a moment?" He jittered about, straightening crooked things and running his finger along the mantel, looking for dust.

She frowned but kept her voice even. "What is it, Daniels?"

"Mr. Collier asked that you review the menu for the buffet tonight." He held out his clipboard for her to inspect, but retained his white-knuckled grip on his notes. His face stayed impassive, except for an occasional tic.

"What buffet?"

"I thought Mrs. Collier would want us to host the Vicar, his wife, and some community leaders before the services tonight, so I took the liberty of inviting them to a light dinner buffet at eight this evening."

Her lips turned down as she glared at the estate manager. "Right. It seems to me that what Mrs. Collier would want is irrelevant, Daniels." She scanned the menu. "Duck à l'orange, lobster, caviar, cranberry salad, a Sacretorte. Not exactly light fare, Daniels."

"Ma'am, it's based on the menu Mrs. Collier approved for the Christmas Eve buffet we sponsored last year at the chapel in the village. I'm sure she'll want us to do something similar this year. I changed some of the side dishes, for variety." He pointed to several lines on the menu.

"Well, I suppose you've already made the arrangements, between Emma and the caterers?"

"Of course, ma'am."

"Then go with it."

He pulled a pen from his shirt pocket. "If you will please initial here, under Mrs. Collier's name, Miss Cassandra? For our records."

Disgust oozed from her, but she scrawled on the menu. "Will Dr. LeClerc and Undersheriff Sondergard be among the invitees?"

"I thought not, ma'am. You know the Vicar's position on *that* kind of people."

That earned him a scowl. "I don't care about the Vicar's prejudices. They're important to the college and good friends. Please see to it that they receive my personal invitation."

"Of course, Miss Cassandra." He turned his rigid, but impassive, features to Brandon. "I trust your quarters are satisfactory, sir?"

Brandon started. "Huh? Oh, sure. They're marvelous! Thank you."

"Will you require further assistance today? James could draw you a bath, or choose appropriate clothing for this evening."

"Really, I'll be fine. I don't want to be a bother."

He sniffed, and his body lurched into what must have been intended as a bow. "With your permission, then, I will leave. I have much to attend to."

Brandon stared at the door. "What was wrong with him? It was almost like he was high on something."

"Humph. High on power, most likely. He's a jerk." She brushed at Brandon's hair. "I was proud of the way you stood up to his insults without being rude back."

He frowned, puzzled. "What insults?"

She shook her head as she stroked his brow. "Poor, innocent Brandon. You'll have to let your Auntie Sandra be your guardian angel. At least you'll get to meet Allen tonight."

"Allen? You mean Dr. LeClerc? Wow, I'd enjoy that. When I knew I was going to take classes from him, I read some of his papers on the canine genome at the University of Chicago library. I'd really like to discuss them with him."

She grinned. "That will make fascinating dinner conversation for the rest of us. He wants to hire you to work in his lab. Did you know that?"

His breath caught in his throat. "Really? In his lab? What a great opportunity!" He let his eyes narrow and stared at her. "You didn't pull any strings on that, did you?"

"Not at all. He looked at your transcript, read the sample term papers and admission essay that you submitted, and said you were what he needed."

"Well, then, I really can't wait to meet him."

"I can't wait either. I'll have to be sure to say something to that damned Vicar and his wife. *That* kind of people, indeed."

Chapter Eleven

"A Hazy Shade of Winter"

Rick glanced at the alarm clock on the mantle in his rooms. *Seven thirty. Plenty of time before the guests start arriving.* He pulled a turtleneck sweater over his head, brushed at his hair, and slid into a pair of loafers. Checking himself one last time in the mirror, he picked up two glasses of white wine from his bar and walked to the door joining his rooms with Brandon's. He knocked, juggling the drinks in one hand. "Brandon? May I come in?"

"Sure, come on in. I'm still in the bathroom." The heavy oak of the door muffled his voice.

Rick entered, and followed the buzz of clippers coming from the direction of the bedroom. "I've got some wine for us. I figured we'd want to fortify ourselves before we go down to face the peasants."

"I better not," Brandon called out. "I don't want to get silly in front of your friends."

Rick found him standing in front of the mirror in his bathroom wearing no shirt and fingering his chin. The clippers he used on his beard rested by the sink. "You won't get silly. It'll just take the edge off meeting these boring people." His eyes raked over Brandon's muscular form. "Mmm, you look nice. Are you going dressed like that?" He handed over the drink.

Brandon took a sip before putting it on the counter top. "I was thinking of shaving off my scruff. What do you think?"

"Don't you dare! I love it!"

"Well, I don't want to embarrass you. Aren't these pretty conventional folks?" He pulled on his shirt. "Should I wear a tie?"

"No tie. They'd think you were being snooty. The beard is fine. I can lend you a sweater, if you want."

"I think I'm good like this." He tucked in his shirt and posed. "How do I look?"

"Like a Jordache model. Where's your stick?"

"Stick?" Brandon looked around the bath.

"Sure, you know. To beat them off with. All the girls, and at least some of the boys, will be breathing down your neck trying to pick you up." He frowned. "Come to think of it, maybe I'm the one who needs the stick, to keep them away from my guy."

Brandon grinned at that. "Don't we kind of have to keep up appearances? The staff acts like Victoria could just pop out through a door any minute."

Rick finished his wine with one long gulp. "I don't want to talk about her. But you're probably right. The Vicar's head would explode if he thought we were a couple. Since it's Christmas, I guess we can give him a break. It'll be our little secret for now."

Brandon snuggled up to him and gave him a kiss. "You're so cute." His fingers pressed against Rick's trousers. "And I'm afraid that's a little *hard* to keep secret."

"I'll have to control myself. I'll just think about Victoria, and it'll shrivel to nothing." He glanced at his watch. "I really should go. Sandra and I will have to greet people and do the host and hostess thing. You don't mind? There's more wine in my rooms. Help yourself."

"No, I understand. I'll mingle. Sandra said Dr. LeClerc was coming. Maybe I can talk to him."

"Yeah, I saw he and his partner got added to the guest list. Daniels took them off because the damned Vicar's been on an anti-gay-marriage crusade, and they've been front and center opposing him. I'm glad Sandra thought to invite them."

"God, what will the Vicar think of us?"

"He'll think you're a house guest staying here. We do that often, and that's all he needs to know." He drained his drink. "I need to head on down. You can show up any time before eight. You know where to go, right? The buffet will be in the West Parlor, just off the foyer. It'll be just a couple dozen people—the town mucky-mucks. The congregation won't get here until after ten."

Brandon nodded and gave him a peck on the cheek. Rick went back to his rooms before entering the hallway. He stopped at the top of the stairs and admired the twenty-foot Yule Tree that now stood in the center of the entry hall. It glimmered with tinsel and lights, and a brilliant crystal star adorned the top. The aromas of duck, dressing, and seafood drifted from the doorway leading into the West Parlor. Daniels bustled out of the Great Hall talking with one of the caterers.

"Looks like your usual outstanding job, Mr. Daniels," he called and ambled down the stairs. "Good work."

"Thank you, sir. The guests should start arriving soon. Miss Cassandra is already in the parlor. Would you care to join her? Perhaps one of the staff could get you some wine?"

"Some Riesling would be nice, thank you. Everything smells wonderful."

"Yes sir. Between our kitchens and the caterers, I think things will work just fine."

Rick sauntered into the parlor, where Sandra sat in a chaise lounge. She wore an elegant gray suit, and had twisted her hair into a French roll. She saluted him with her wineglass. "Hi. Where's Brandon?"

"He's still getting ready. You look lovely. Like Kim Novak in *Vertigo*, except your hair isn't platinum blonde."

"I don't quite have the figure to match, either." The doorbell chimed. "I guess that's our cue." She heaved a sigh and rose to her feet.

They walked together to the entry, where James was helping a pudgy, middle-aged couple with their wraps. Rick extended his hand. "Vicar Teague, how nice to see you. Rachel, you too."

The Vicar pumped his hand like a mechanic jacking up a car to fix a flat. "Rick. It's so good of you to help out our parish like this. God bless you."

Rachel's hand was a limp dishrag in his palm after the Vicar's crushing grip. "You're doing the Lord's work tonight, that's for sure Rick. Your manor is beautiful, as always. My compliments to Daniels." She bestowed a cherubic smile on him while gazing about. "Oh dear, are we the first ones here?"

Sandra clasped her hand. "Vicar and Mrs. Teague, I'm so glad you're here. You can help us greet the other guests."

The door chimed again, and a gaggle of persons from the village filled the foyer. Rick busied himself with James, assisting with coats, letting Sandra, Rachel and the Vicar greet people and lead them to the parlor.

The Vicar hovered at Rick's side. When the last of the arrivals were in the parlor and had drinks in hand, he leaned in and whispered, "Will your delightful wife be returning from her European adventure for the holidays?"

Rick's face flushed, but he managed to get out, "She decided to stay in Europe. Apparently this is a good time to visit the museums, to study the masters. No tourists."

"Ah. I wish I had her talent. Still, it must be difficult for you with her being gone at this time for families."

Rick gritted his teeth. "Well, I wouldn't want to stand in the way of her artistic ambitions."

The Vicar *tsked*. "Of course. She's fortunate you are so understanding. Mrs. Teague and I always include both of you in our prayers."

"I appreciate that, Vicar." Rick glanced at the foyer and plotted his escape. "Will you excuse me? I see the last of our dinner guests have arrived."

He beamed as he recognized the two young men standing in the foyer. "Dr. LeClerc and Undersheriff Sondergard. It's wonderful to see you again. Thanks for coming."

LeClerc grinned back and shook his hand. "Thanks for having us. It's always a pleasure. You and Sandra are so helpful to the College."

Sondergard handed his coat to James and shook hands with Rick. "Good evening. The place looks great."

"Thank you. Daniels did a great job. Won't you join us in the parlor?" Movement on the stairs caught his eye, and he broke into a happy smile. "Brandon! Come here and meet Dr. LeClerc and his partner, Undersheriff Sondergard."

"Dr. LeClerc! I'm honored! I'm going to be one of your students this spring." Brandon trotted down the stairs to shake hands with the couple.

LeClerc frowned. "Brandon...you wouldn't be the new transfer student from Chicago? The one who got the Montgomery Fellowship?"

Brandon's face turned crimson. "That's me."

"Congratulations! You have very impressive credentials. I never expected to meet you tonight." He pulled Brandon to one side. "Say, would you be interested in working in my lab? That term paper you wrote comparing the amino acid sequences in measles and canine distemper was really impressive. I'm working on a similar project you might be interested in." The two wandered off together to the parlor, speaking a language that may as well have been Sanskrit to Rick's ears.

Sondergard chuckled. "I guess they'll be busy for the rest of night." He lowered his voice. "I hate to trouble you, but do you have a moment?"

"Sure. Do we need to go my study?"

"No, this will be fine. I don't know if Daniels has spoken to you, but there's been some trespassing problems on the estate this fall. Twice now, I've gotten calls and had to chase kids out of your old carriage house."

Rick paled. "That's not good." Despite his efforts to suppress them, memories of Victoria and the old carriage house coiled like a serpent in the pit of his stomach and threatened to poison the peace of this evening. He fought to keep his voice steady. "I know Daniels stores maintenance things there—pesticides and other stuff that isn't safe unless you know what you're doing. And Victoria fired the contractors halfway through the renovation of the place last winter, so who knows if it's structurally sound. The floors might collapse or something." He raked his fingers through his hair.

Sam nodded. "That's what I thought, too. These are good kids, mostly, just sneaking around looking for a place to smoke some weed and maybe make out. But I thought you should know."

"How did they get in? We have a fence, after all."

"The ice storm last year tore it up pretty bad in spots. There's several places you can just walk right onto the estate. I spoke to Daniels, but he said his budget didn't include a new fence."

"Nonsense. We can't have these kids wandering around those chemicals. I'll speak to him and we'll get that fixed."

"Thanks, Rick. I knew I could depend on you." His eyes narrowed. "How are you doing, sir? Is there anything I can do for you?"

"No, no. Thank you, Sam. I really appreciated your help, and your discretion, last spring when Victoria left with all that money. It could have damaged the bank financially if it had gotten out. I won't forget your help."

"No problem, Rick. It's all part of my job. You and Sandra didn't want to press charges over the missing funds, so there was no reason to make a public fuss about it. If you want, I could recommend a private investigator. I'm sure we could track her down, and the one I have in mind would be discreet."

"I don't think so, Sam, but thanks anyway." He heaved a tremulous sigh. "If she wants to disappear, it seems to me she has that right. And who knows, maybe she'll turn up one day."

The voices in the next room hushed, and the Vicar's blessing hovered over them. Rick lowered his eyes and used the opportunity to calm the anxiety churning in his stomach. *Sweet Jesus. In the carriage house, no less.*

Once the prayer finished, he entered the parlor and his gaze roved over his gathered friends and acquaintances. Most stood in two efficient serving lines at the buffet, and a few already sat at the round-topped banquet tables scattered about the room. *I'll have to admit Daniels is efficient.*

The Vicar's wife broke off a conversation with a member of the Village Council and bustled over to him. "Rick, please be sure to thank Daniels for all his work tonight. He's such a perfect angel."

"Glad to help, Rachel. Are your children coming back for the holidays?"

"Yes. You know, Mark, our oldest, spent the fall in California on a Mission, working with Rick Warren?"

"Warren? I think I've heard of him."

"He's pastor at Saddleback Church. There was a presidential debate there last fall. Senator McCain did such a marvelous job addressing the issues Christians care about, don't you think?"

"Mmm. So what was your son doing out there? Charity work for the church?"

"Oh no, something much more important. He worked on the campaign to save marriage—and praise the Lord, we won!" She beamed at him.

He let his lips turn down. "You mean Proposition Eight. I'm sorry, but I never quite saw how two men getting married threatened anyone else's marriage."

She scowled at him. "It's in the Bible. That court decision in California was the work of Satan." Her eyes narrowed and she peered at him. "But thanks to our prayers and hard work, God's will prevailed. Before the election, the Vicar gave several sermons on how good Christians think about the moral issues facing our country and how we should vote. I'm sure he'd be glad to send you copies."

"I don't think that will be necessary, thank you." His eyes gazed the room and lit on Brandon and Allen LeClerc huddled in a corner. "If you'll excuse me, I see someone I need to speak with."

He worked his way through the room to where the pair stood, still discussing genetics. "I see the two of you are hard at work."

LeClerc gave him a blank look before seeming to reorient himself to casual conversation. "This is quite a bright young man we've got here, Rick. I understand he's staying at the estate while he's in school? That's very generous of you."

Brandon turned crimson and his eyes lit with excitement. "He's invited me to work in his genetics lab. I can't wait. I'm going to drive up to the college on Monday for a tour. Do you know what he's *doing* there?"

"We get regular reports at the Regents' meetings." He grinned at LeClerc. "I just wish they were in English instead of science-ese. But, yes, I have a general idea. We're very fortunate to have someone of Allen's stature at Montgomery College." He tipped his head toward the serving lines. "You really should get some food before it's all gone."

LeClerc chuckled. "We got so involved talking about our research, I'm afraid we forgot. Thanks for reminding us. Brandon, would you like to sit with Sam and me? I'd like you to meet my better half."

"Sure. Unless..." He raised his eyebrows and looked at Rick. "Would you like me to sit with you and Sandra?"

"No, that's fine. It's good for the two of you to get to know each other. I'm glad that you've hit it off, and that you'll have a position in our most distinguished research lab. Allen, I trust you and Sam will take good care of him—keep the vultures away."

"If you mean the Vicar and his wife, we can handle them just fine. Come on Brandon."

He watched them walk together to the buffet when Sandra's arm hooked through his. "They seem to have hit it off," she whispered.

He looked at Brandon shaking hands with Sam Sondergard in the serving line. "Truly. I wonder if this is how a parent feels when they send a child off to college?"

"Proud and kind of wistful?"

He shook his head. "I was thinking more like old."

"You are robbing the cradle a bit." She squeezed his arm. "But I'm glad for both of you. Are you going to eat?"

"Yes, but I thought I'd wait until everyone else was seated."

"Me, too. I saw you speaking to the Vicar's wife just now."

He frowned at that. "I swear, I've just about had it with her, and the Vicar, too. She told me he gave sermons all fall about how 'good Christians' should vote. I've half a mind to turn them in to the IRS and let the church lose its tax-exempt status."

"I know what you mean. Daniels left Allen and Sam off the invitation list because those two are so hateful to gay people. I'm going to rub their noses in it sometime tonight. I just haven't had the chance yet."

"Well, she and I had words already, about what happened in California."

"Good for you. I was going to parade Allen and Sam in front of them, but that's using our friends to make a point. This is better. I guess I'll drop it, for tonight anyway."

"Good idea. Oh, one more thing before we mingle. Shall the three of us have breakfast together in the morning? The staff has the day off, but I'm sure Brandon and I can whomp something up in the kitchen. We could do our gift exchange, and then eat. We might even all drive in to Dubuque and catch a movie."

"That sounds wonderful, especially since that damned Daniels turned our Christmas Eve into a social event. What time?"

"I'll give you a ring when we get up. Probably around nine or so?"

"That works for me. I think Brandon will like my gift." She gave him a Cheshire grin and sashayed to the serving line before he could speak.

Chapter Twelve

"Have Yourself a Merry Little Christmas"

Sunlight streaming through the windows of Rick's bedroom pulled Brandon from his dreams. Next to him Rick snuffled and stirred in his sleep before settling into a gentle snore. Brandon smiled and placed a soft kiss on his lover's cheek, threw off his covers, and stretched. Without bothering to dress, he picked up the clothes scattered about the room and folded them over a chair near the fireplace. Glancing at the darkened Yule tree, he switched on the lights. *Wouldn't do to have a dark tree on Christmas morning. Someone sure did a fantastic job decorating it.* A faint pang of disappointment tinged the thought: he'd had visions that the two of them would do that together.

A coffeemaker on the bar caught his attention. Before long, the scents of Jamaican Blue Mountain and the sounds of liquid gurgling filled the room. While it finished brewing, he retrieved his clothes and walked on silent feet to his rooms, where he refreshed himself in his bath. Someone, perhaps James, had left a plush, maroon robe draped over a chair in his bedroom. After slipping into the robe, he pulled the sheets back on his bed and mussed them as though he'd slept in it the night before.

"What are you doing?" Rick stood in the doorway wearing a matching robe and holding two steaming mugs. A sly smile trifled with his lips.

"Making it look like I slept here last night. Shouldn't we keep up appearances, for the servants?"

Rick handed him one of the mugs and planted a kiss on his cheek. "That's not necessary. In the first place, they're not servants. They're contractors from our hotel in town, and they only come here once a week. In the second place, they don't have a clue who's supposed to be sleeping where. We keep several rooms ready for drop-in guests, and they put up fresh linens once a week, regardless." He smiled. "And in the third place, they work for us, not the other way around. It doesn't matter what they think. Thanks for starting the coffee, by the way."

"Thanks for bringing me a cup." Brandon sipped his. "Just like I like it."

"You bet. Why don't we take our showers and go downstairs? I'll call Sandra, and we can cook omelets or something."

"Sounds good. I know a recipe for a baked pancake that I used to fix for...that I used to fix. You'll have to lead me to the kitchen. It wasn't on Sandra's tour yesterday."

"What a surprise. Cooking isn't one of her charms." He gulped at his coffee. "Let's get ready. The weather's supposed to be nice today, all the way up to fifty. Maybe we can do a walking tour of the grounds later."

Less than an hour later, Brandon pulled the glass pie plate from the oven and poured pancake batter over the melted butter covering the surface. He slipped the concoction back into the oven and set the timer. "It'll be ready in about thirty minutes. I'll need to dust it with powdered sugar when it comes out."

"It looks delicious. Check the pantry for the sugar—I'm sure there's some there." Rick stood at the island in the kitchen, chopping scallions, green onions, mushrooms, and ham for the omelets. An array of copper-bottomed pans hung over his head, suspended from a rack in the ceiling. Sun streamed through the windows that looked out onto the rear patio.

"I see it. Anything I can do to help?"

"Jasper's scratching at the door. Would you let him back in? And maybe feed him and freshen his water?"

"Sure. He's a nice dog."

"He's friendly, all right. I'm afraid he misses Victoria. He was her constant companion, even though Daniels is the one who usually takes care of him."

Brandon scooped food from a can into Jasper's bowl and filled his water bowl. "That's a good dog!" Jasper paused to gaze at him and wag his tail before he resumed his discreet gobbling. "What else can I do?"

Rick nodded to a bright alcove that extruded from the kitchen. "You could set the table, if you want. The dishes are in that cabinet over there."

"Good morning, everyone." A somewhat disheveled Sandra ambled into the room, yawning and pushing at her hair. She wore a pink robe and fluffy, white bunny slippers. "I need caffeine." She plopped down in the dining alcove while Brandon poured her a cup.

"Do you take anything in it?"

"There's sweetener here at the table. Just bring me the cup and a spoon. That's a dear." She eyed the four brightly wrapped packages on the table. "I see Santa's already been here."

Brandon served her coffee and grinned. "I didn't know what to do for the two of you. I hope you like it."

"Honey, coffee in the morning is the only gift I really need. It's sweet that you thought of us. I'm sure we'll love whatever you bought." She added two more small packages to the table. "There. Now we're all set." She lounged back and sipped at the steaming brew.

Rick called out from where he stood at the island. "Brandon's fixing us a baked pancake, and I'm getting omelets ready. You want one?"

She looked at her waistline and sighed. "I shouldn't. It'll play havoc with my girlish figure."

Brandon settled across from her at the table with a glass of orange juice. "It's Christmas. Treat yourself. Besides, your figure is perfect."

"You're a darling." She reached out. "Touch my hand."

Puzzled, he stroked her offered palm.

"Ouch! Rick, your little friend here twisted my *arm!* Now I just have to have an omelet and a pancake!"

Brandon chuckled. "You're so funny."

"That's me, comedienne extraordinaire." Her eyes sparkled at him. "I'm so glad you're here. Did you have a good conversation with Allen last night?"

"You mean Dr. LeClerc? Yes! He's so nice, and I'm looking forward to working in his lab. Uh, Rick? He and Sam asked the three of us to dinner at their home next Tuesday night. I told them I'd have to check with the two of you."

"That sounds like fun. You'll get to meet their dog, Teena. She's pretty special." Rick stood in the doorway, sipping apple juice. "Shall we open presents now while we wait for the pancake to cook?"

Sandra beamed at him. "That sounds divine! I'll play Santa and hand out the gifts."

Brandon waited to open his two packages, watching the others.

Sandra tore the wrapping off the box from him. "Look! It's running shoes!"

"I just used a box I got from the store. I wouldn't give you shoes for Christmas!"

"I knew that, dear." She lifted the lid and removed the red and green tissue paper to reveal a scarf and mittens, knitted in a complex cable pattern with gold and brown yarn.

"Brandon, this is beautiful! And the colors are perfect!" She held the scarf next to her cheek. "It's so soft. This must have cost you a fortune!"

Brandon's face heated. "It's alpaca. A friend at the library sold me the yarn at cost, so I didn't have to spend very much on it."

Rick opened his box to reveal a scarf and gloves, from similar yarn but in sepia and blue. "Brandon, this is incredible. Did you say *yarn?* You mean you *knitted* these?"

"Well, yeah. They gave free classes at the library. The scarves were easy, but Hilda had to help with the mittens and gloves. Are they all right?"

"They're magnificent! And even more so since you made them yourself!" Sandra jumped up from her seat and ran to give him a sloppy kiss on his forehead. "You're just full of surprises."

Rick nodded. "You sure are." He fingered his gift. "You know, I tried to learn how once. The doctor said it would relieve stress, but I could never figure it out. The only thing I can knit is my eyebrows. Thank you. This is beautiful, and just what I need for those cold winter days, here and in Chicago."

Sandra and Rick opened their gifts to each other—onyx cufflinks for Rick and pearl earrings for Sandra.

"Brandon, honey, you haven't opened your gifts from us. You've got to do mine last!" She nudged the packages toward him.

"Okay. I was worried you might not like what I did for you." Brandon tore the tape off the end of Rick's gift and slipped the box out of the wrapping. "Oh my God, it's a notebook computer!"

"It's an android tablet, the latest thing from France in portable devices. I thought you could use it for classes this spring."

"Rick, thank you! I looked at these, but didn't see how I could quite stretch my financial aid to get one. It's perfect!"

"I had the tech at the bank install Open Office for you, so you'll have a word processor, spreadsheets, everything you'll need for school. We can connect it to the wireless network here in the house."

Sandra grinned. "That's just what you need, Brandon! You can use it in the Writing Room when you set it up as your study." She pushed the last, small box to him. "Okay, now open my gift to you."

Brandon tugged at the ribbon and tore the wrapping off. He opened the little box to reveal a set of car keys. He raised astonished eyes to gaze at Sandra. "What's this?"

"I got you a car, honey. So you can drive back and forth to classes. It's a new Prius, to save on gas and be friendly to the environment."

"Sandra, I don't know what to say!"

"Just say 'thank you, Sandra.' I put it in both our names, so you won't have to worry about insurance or taxes or anything. So I guess it's just half a car. But it's for you."

"Thank you, Sandra. It just seems like so much."

"I've got the money, and I thought a touch of independence for you would be a good thing. This way if Rick needs to run back to Chicago, he can use that tank of an SUV that he drives and you'll still have transportation here. It's parked out front, in the circle drive. I stayed up last night and moved it from the garage after everyone left. Let's go look! It's red. I hope you like the color."

"I'm sure it's perfect. Uh, can someone stay back and take the pancake out? It's almost time."

Rick stood. "You two go admire your new toy. I'll stay here and start the omelets and bacon. What do I do when the timer goes off?"

"Just take it out, put it on a trivet, and dust it with powdered sugar. It'll be all poofy. We'll be right back." Sandra wrapped her new scarf about her neck, grabbed his hand, and they rushed from the room.

Brandon stood with his hands on his hips and surveyed the Writing Room. Porcelain knickknacks stood scattered on the otherwise empty bookshelves. The afternoon sunlight relieved the interior's gloomy dark paneling and oak floors. The desk was more of a delicate table than a useful workspace; it made Brandon think of powdered wigs and Marie Antoinette. He plopped down in the plush chair behind it and plugged in his new computer before examining his new workspace. *At least it's got some drawers for storage.* A leather folder lay open on the desk alongside a Mont Blanc fountain pen and an art deco statue of Eros. The letters *VMC* blazed in red script from the stationery resting inside the folder. *VMC — Victoria Montgomery Collier.*

His gaze turned to the three boxes he'd carried down from his rooms upstairs. He sighed and contemplated the task of rearranging the knickknacks on the shelves and unpacking his books. After a moment of reflection, he decided to put all of the statuettes from one bookcase on the desk and rearrange them after he finished with his books. Taking care, he shuttled back and forth until the desktop was a forest of gleaming figurines. As he placed the final one on the crowded surface, he gave it a little push to keep it away from the edge. The figure's base caught on the leather notebook, which in turn pushed against the statue of Eros. It tottered for a moment on the lip of the desk. He snatched at it, but was too late. The tinkle of shattering porcelain twisted at his guts. "Fuck me! Now I've done it."

He stared in dismay at the little statue, now scattered in several glittering pieces on the hardwood floor. "What'll I do?" He looked around, picked up a piece of Victoria's stationery, and used it as a dustpan to sweep up the shards. The bottom drawer of the desk looked large enough, so he jerked it open, pushed the contents inside to the front, and dumped the remains of Eros in the back. While he was on his hands and knees, his eyes caught a set of keys reading *Lindermont Arms Apartments* with a Dubuque address hanging from the rear panel of the desk. They were in the well of the drawer and out of sight unless the drawer was open and someone occupied his present position. He was too flustered to wonder about hidden keys, though, with the shattered statue accusing him. He shoved papers and other things inside toward the back, hiding the shards. *Maybe I can replace it before anyone notices.*

"You need help in here?"

Brandon's heart stopped, and he looked up to see Rick standing in the doorway. "Uh, no. I was just going to un-box my books. I wasn't sure what to do with these knickknacks."

Rick grinned. "Victoria's head would explode if she heard you call them that. They're her little treasures. God knows what she spent on them." He shrugged. "Don't worry about it. Just put them anywhere. We can have Daniels box them up next week. How about you take a break and we walk around the grounds? It's nice out, and we might not have another opportunity until spring."

"Sure. That sounds like fun." Brandon checked to make sure he'd shut the drawer before following Rick down the hall to the foyer.

As they were donning their coats, Jasper trotted down the stairs and sniffled at Rick's hand. "Hey, fella. Do you need to go outside again?" The dog stared at him with soulful eyes and woofed. Rick glanced at Brandon. "There's a leash in the coatroom. Would you mind handing it to me?" He knelt and tousled the animal's ears. "Yeah, you're a good dog. We'll take care of you."

Outside, Brandon gazed over the front lawn. "The snow's all melted. You hardly need your scarf today."

"I wanted to wear it anyway. Thank you again. This is a wonderful gift, made with your own hands."

"You're welcome. It's nothing, compared to everything you've done for me. So, where are we going?"

"I just thought we'd walk around." He pointed down the hill. "In the spring, this whole area is covered with tulips, lilies, and hyacinths. We'll open the place up to the public."

"It sounds beautiful. I think Peter mentioned it to me once."

"Yeah. Sometimes we have a picnic for the special customers at the bank. Last time, we opened up the Manor and we must have had twenty houseguests, plus another forty or so who stayed at the motel in town. The Board's talked about doing it again this spring as kind of a confidence builder that won't cost them much."

"Well, just let me know if I need to disappear or anything. I wouldn't want to be in the way."

"Don't be silly. You can help host it, assuming you have time, what with school and all. Come on. Let's follow the drive and you can see some of the old out-buildings on the estate, back when it was a working farm."

Brandon paused in front of his new, bright red car that was still sitting in the drive. "I can't believe she did this. Want to go on another test drive after our walkabout?"

Rick grinned. "Sure. Maybe we can all go out and look at Christmas lights tonight. Sandra is a bit over-the-top sometimes, but her heart's in the right place. It'll sure be convenient for you to have your own car. I was thinking you could use the estate's jeep, but that would mean sharing with Daniels. She's right. This is a better solution."

Brandon followed him down the drive and back up the hill. At the top, where he had first seen the Manor yesterday, he turned and looked back. "I can't believe I'm going to be living there."

"It's huge, all right. But you'll get used to it."

"I meant, I can't believe I'll be living with you. It's like a dream come true."

"For me, too." A cell phone buzzed, and Rick felt inside his coat. "Damn, it's mine. Take the leash, will you? I bet it's my sister." He flipped it open and read the screen. "Yup. This'll take a few minutes."

Brandon let Jasper tug him on down the road, ahead of Rick. Despite the warm, sunny weather, snow still clustered in clumps in the undergrowth of the forest. Beyond the Manor's manicured boundaries, the rest of the estate was a tangled wildwood. Jasper stopped now and then to sniff at a leaf before dashing off to follow some scent. Brandon trotted after, letting the dog lead him forward. Before long, they reached the Y junction in the road, and Jasper took the graveled route that led to the old carriage house.

A few hundred feet down the road, the dog yelped and jerked on his leash. Brandon stumbled at the unexpected lurch and the leather strap slipped from his fingers. "Damn! Jasper! Come back here!" The dog disappeared around a bend, and frantic barks echoed through the forest. Brandon broke into a run and spied an old, two-story stone building resting at the end of the roadway. Jasper stood on his hind legs at the door, his claws scrabbling at the surface while he barked.

"Jasper, fella, what's wrong?" Brandon trotted up to him and stroked the animal's back. "It's all right. Do you want in there?" He wrapped the leash around his wrist so that the dog couldn't escape and tested the door. "It's unlocked. Let's see what the problem is."

Beams of sunlight slanted through the interior like smoky lasers. Sawhorses and tools lay scattered about, along with spent rubbers, beer cans, and cigarette butts. A chemical smell oozed from sacks of pesticide and fertilizer piled in one corner, mixing with the fetid scent of urine and garbage that permeated the air. Hoes, shovels and scythes hung from the bare rafters. Unpainted plasterboard covered some of the walls. The wounds of unfinished construction left the insides of other walls exposed in lath, plaster, and framing. Jasper pulled him forward toward a door on the opposite side of the room. The floor creaked and yielded under his weight as he edged through the debris. "Jasper, hold up, boy. I'm not sure it's safe in here."

"What do you think you're doing?" Rick's voice rapped at him from the doorway.

Brandon turned. "Jasper led me here. He went crazy at the door, so I thought we'd check it out."

"Well, you shouldn't be in here. It's not safe." He scowled. "Watch the floor. There's an old gravity furnace in the basement from back when the chauffeur used to live here. There's even still coal down there, God knows why. Anyway, the contractor told me everything's all rotted out. I don't know why Daniels doesn't keep this place locked up." He kicked a crumpled beer can to one side and snorted. "We should just take that damned dog and get out of here."

"Sure, whatever you say. Come on, Jasper." Brandon tugged at the leash and pulled a reluctant Jasper to the door. He peered at Rick's rigid face. "Don't be mad, okay?"

"Just stay away from here. It's full of all that fertilizer and pesticide, and the floors need to be rebuilt. It's not safe." He toed at the rubbers and beer cans on the floor. "Look at this mess. The Sheriff told me kids from the village were hanging out here. I had no idea it would be so disgusting."

"I could clean it up, if you want."

Rick didn't look at him. "Don't be stupid. That's what Daniels is for. Let's just get out of here." He waited for Brandon to leave, slammed the door shut, and stalked off without another word.

Stricken, Brandon followed in silence.

Chapter Thirteen

"Every Rose Has Its Thorn"

The dumbbell clanged against the floor and Rick's biceps burned with an inner fire. Sweat stung his eyes, and he swiped at his brow with a towel before sprawling on the floor. Heaving a sigh, he counted out fifty leg lifts and another fifty crunches.

Steam wafted from the hot tub on the other side of the glass wall dividing his gym from Lindermont's indoor swimming pool. His muscles ached, but he resisted the temptation to relax in the inviting waters. *Two more circuits and I'm done. God, I hate working out alone.* He clambered to his feet and started over again with squats. His exercises kept cadence with a mindless *Best of the Bee Gees* CD pounding from the overhead speakers.

He stared at the Nautilus machine and contemplated bench presses. *It cost enough, but at least you don't need a spotter.* He winced, remembering Sandra's biting words when she'd caught him working out alone last summer. *It's not like I was trying to kill myself, but I have to admit bench presses with a barbell, by yourself, are pretty reckless.* He shuddered, settled under the bars, edged into position, and fixated on the exercise. Motion, resistance, and breathing suffused his thoughts as his body triumphed over the power of the machine. He jumped when a voice penetrated his concentration.

"Hi! Would you like me to spot you?" Brandon stood at his feet, a silly grin on his face, wearing a crisp white T-shirt and faded, blue gym shorts. "James told me you were here when I got back from the college, so I changed into workout duds and thought I'd join in."

Rick sat up and swept the back of his hand across his forehead. "Hey, you. Nah, I'm almost done." He stood and picked up a dumbbell. "How was your first visit to campus? What did you think of Allen's lab?"

Brandon draped his towel over the Nautilus bench and started his stretching routine. "It was fantastic! I'd only read about most of the equipment he'd gotten, but I actually got to touch it today. He gave me the syllabus for his course too. I've got a pre-class paper I'll have to write. Then we talked about the research project I'll be working on, and I filled out some paperwork for him."

"I thought the business offices were closed for the holiday break?" Rick balanced on one leg and counted out calf raises.

"They are, but you can't shut down a lab like Dr. LeClerc's for two weeks. There are ongoing experiments, and the animals need attention too. He said I could turn in the paperwork after the first of the year and start in the lab before classes begin." He flopped to the floor and snapped out two dozen quick crunches.

"Sounds like you're looking forward to it."

"You bet. This is the opportunity of a lifetime. And it's all because of you. I won't forget it."

Rick's lips tugged downward on his face. "All I did was suggest you apply. You earned everything else."

"And gave me a place to live." Brandon's eyes glowed as they swept over Rick's sweat-drenched form. "And then there's that other thing you do for me."

"I'd say that other thing is more or less mutual." Rick glanced at his watch. "Shit, I'm running behind and I really wanted to unwind for a few minutes in the hot tub. You want to join me?"

"I really should spend a few minutes working out. I don't want to get flabby—what would my boyfriend think?" He winked. "What time do your sister and her husband get here?"

"Shouldn't be until this evening. But with Molly, you never know." Rick slipped off his soggy T-shirt and headed toward the showers. "I think we've got some time to relax beforehand, if you catch my drift."

Brandon grinned. "I'll hurry through my exercises. Meet in your room, maybe?"

"Sounds good, unless you want to join me in the hot tub first?"

"No, I really need to work out, and then I want to shower and smell good for you. Stinky sex sucks."

"I don't know. Some people prefer stinky sex. Besides, I like the way you smell."

Rick left the door to Brandon's rooms open so he could listen for when the shower turned off. At that cue, he put a CD of Ashkenazy playing Rachmaninov on the stereo and pulled a pitcher of iced chai from the refrigerator in his bar. The maid service came on Mondays, and fresh sheets beckoned. He tugged at the belt on his robe, grinned, and lounged on the bed, waiting.

His heart quickened as Brandon appeared in the doorway, a towel wrapped about his slim waist and his hair a tousled mat of fire atop his head. "You look lovely. There's some chai at the bar, if you'd like a drink."

"Thanks." Brandon poured a glass while his eyes raked over Rick, seeming to devour his body from head to toe. "You look scrumptious."

Rick let a sly smile sneak across his lips as heat coiled from his stomach and flared out his loins. "God, I never tire of looking at you."

A grin flashed across Brandon's features, and he flexed his abs while twisting his hips. "You're not so bad yourself, you know. But I'm glad you like looking." His sudden erection lifted the towel at his waist, and his fingers scrambled to strip it off.

Rick sat on the edge of the bed and untied the belt on his robe. "Come here. I need to snuggle."

Brandon let the towel drop to the floor and he hurried across the room, naked, a glass of chai in one hand. "You snuggle good."

Before the two could embrace, the phone emitted a shrill demand for attention. Rick scowled at it and muttered, "What could that be?"

"Don't answer." Brandon's tongue traced a moist trail up Rick's neck, from his shoulder to his ear.

"God, that's different. Your tongue's still cold from the drink." He eyed the phone as it continued to ring. "I should answer. It might be Molly." He picked up the handset. "Hello?"

Daniels' precise voice came from the other end. "Sir, something has come up regarding the cleaning crew this morning."

Irritation flushed his face. "So handle it, Daniels. That's your job."

"Yes, sir. But James felt that I should speak to you first."

"James wanted you to speak to me?" Rick frowned. "Meet me in fifteen minutes in my study." He slammed the phone back into its cradle.

Brandon's lips caressed Rick's nipple, and his fingers reached between his legs. Can't it wait?"

Rick pushed him away. "I'm sorry. If it were just Daniels, I'd tell him to go fuck himself. But if James thinks I need to be involved, that means Daniels is planning something nasty that I need to veto. Whatever it is, I'll attend to it and come right back." He stood and walked to the closet, where he tossed his robe on the floor and pulled on a clean shirt.

"I'll go with you, if that's all right."

"Whatever. You could stay here and keep the bed warm for us if you want."

"I don't mind." Brandon hopped to his feet and raced to his room. "Don't leave without me!"

Rick tugged on a pair of chinos and pulled penny loafers from the shoe rack. He thought about socks, but then decided not to bother. He glanced at the door to Brandon's room. *He probably thinks whatever it is won't take as long if he's along.* "Are you coming?"

Brandon appeared with his shirt fluttering behind him, his hair slicked back and flip-flops on his feet. "I'm almost ready." His fingers tore at the buttons.

Rick's eyes lingered on the little red hairs that curled on each of Brandon's exposed toes. "Uh, grab a pair of my loafers, okay? Flip-flops aren't really what a Manor guest should wear."

Brandon stuffed his shirt into his blue jeans and rummaged in Rick's closet. "Thanks." He slipped into the shoes. "Convenient we're the same size. Let's get this over with so we can get back to what we were doing."

Daniels and James already were hovering outside Rick's study when they arrived. Rick waved them inside and positioned himself behind the ornate Victorian desk his father-in-law had bequeathed him. The two employees stood on the other side, while Brandon wandered over to the bookcase and seemed to browse the titles on the shelves.

Rick grimaced and glared at Daniels. "All right, what's so blasted important that you have to bother me right this instant?"

His face jerked in a tic. "It has to do with the cleaning crew, sir. They have stolen one of Mrs. Collier's statuettes."

"You are certain of this? You have a witness?"

"No, sir. But it was here last week, and it's gone now. After they left this morning, I did my usual follow-up to be sure they'd not taken any shortcuts cleaning. I paid special attention to Mrs. Collier's study, since Master Brandon will be using it during his stay. That's when I saw the statuette was missing."

"So what knickknack, exactly, is missing?"

"It's a statuette of Eros, sir. It's one of Mrs. Collier's favorites."

"I think I recall it. That's the Moreau original, isn't it? A grotesque little thing."

Brandon dropped his book with a thump, but didn't say anything as he knelt to recover it.

Daniels rolled his eyes and glanced at Brandon before turning back to Rick. "That's the one, sir." The fingers of one hand crawled like spiders over the back of the other, scratching like a cat on one's favorite furniture.

God, he's itched himself raw. Why is he so nervous? Rick turned his gaze to James. "Why do you think this needs my attention?"

"Daniels thinks we should insist the contractor fire everyone who cleaned at the Manor today. There's no basis for that, sir. It could just be misplaced."

Rick turned a narrowed gaze to Daniels. "Is that true? That you want them all fired?"

"Yes, sir. They shouldn't get by with it."

"That's a bit drastic, don't you think? I'd have to check the inventory, but I doubt this costed all that much money."

"Mrs. Collier paid over four hundred pounds for it when she was in London two years ago, sir. But that's not the point. We can't permit them to steal from us."

"But we don't know they did that, do we, Daniels? How many people were here from the church, less than a week ago? It could be one of them. Or, as James points out, it could be just misplaced."

"Sir, no one from our church would steal. And moreover, I still think...."

"It's what I think that matters, Daniels. We've been happy with this service, haven't we?"

"Yes, sir."

James piped up, "They've been with us for over five years, and it's mostly all the same people who come very week. They're good folks."

"Yes, well then. Unless there's another incident, just write it off on the inventory. We can afford it."

"But sir, what will I tell Mrs. Collier when she returns? This was one of her favorites."

Darkness slithered into his gut at the mention of Victoria's possible return. "You let me worry about Mrs. Collier," he snapped. "James, thank you for bringing this to my attention. Is there anything else?" He used his eyes to throw icy daggers at Daniels.

"No, sir."

"I've got one more thing while you're here. What's your progress on getting the fence repaired?"

"I spoke to a contractor in Dubuque, sir. He says that they can't do it in the winter. The ground's frozen, and they can't properly seat the posts."

"Can't they put a temporary fence up or something? I don't want kids getting hurt on the estate."

"I'll look into it, sir. It will add to the expense, and it won't be as secure."

"I told you I didn't care about the damned expense. Take care of it." He shuffled papers on his desk and scowled. "Now get out of here. My sister and her husband will be here tonight. Make sure that rooms are ready for them. In the west wing, where they can have some privacy."

Daniels' eyes danced a nervous jitterbug around the room, settling for a moment where Brandon huddled in the shadows. "Whatever you say, sir." He followed James out of the room, closing the door as he left.

Rick stared at his desktop and swore under his breath. He jumped when Brandon spoke.

"That was, uh, interesting."

"I almost forgot you were here. That son of a bitch would have fired them all, right at the holidays, if James hadn't had the good sense to call me in. Sometimes I wish I could just get rid of the bastard."

Brandon retreated further into the darkness next to the bookcases. He looked at his shoes and stammered, "Uh, I have a confession to make."

Rick peered at him. "Is there something wrong?"

"Well, I think I know what happened to that statue. I'm so sorry."

"Whatever it is, I'm sure it'll be all right."

Brandon heaved a sigh. "You know, Sandra suggested I use Victoria's, I mean Mrs. Collier's, study? And you said it was okay."

"Of course. No sense in it going to waste."

"So, I took my books down there. When I was rearranging things, this one little porcelain statue fell and broke on the floor."

"Ah! What did you do with the pieces?"

"I swept them up and hid them in the desk. I was thinking I'd glue it together or something."

Well, that solves our little mystery. Why didn't you say something?"

"I don't know. I was mortified, as if I'd destroyed something of *hers* on purpose, even though it was an accident. Like I said, I was going to try to glue it back together, or find a replacement, before anyone noticed. I'm sure the pieces are still there."

Rick shook his head. "I meant, why didn't you speak up just now? If I hadn't intervened, a bunch of people could have lost their jobs over this."

"I know. I'm sorry. I would have said something before I let him fire them." Clouds shifted outdoors, and a beam of sunlight flashed across his face. "I'm such an idiot. You must hate me."

"I don't hate you, but this is all pretty silly. You'll need to tell Daniels what happened before he accuses the cleaning people." He reached for the phone.

Brandon's face turned ashen. "Oh God, don't make me tell him. He makes me feel like I'm ten years old and I just wet my pants in front of everyone."

Rick's hand lingered on the handset. "He has to know."

"Can't you tell him? Please? I'll make it up to you." A halfhearted grin trembled on his features, but tears glimmered in his eyes.

"Really, if you're going to live here, you have to learn how to deal with the hired help." Rick's fingers drummed on the phone before he picked it up and dialed a number. "Daniels. Brandon just told me he remembers breaking a statue when he moved his books into the study. You'll find the shards in the desk in one of the drawers...." He raised his eyebrows and glanced at Brandon.

"The lower right-hand drawer, in the back."

"He says in the lower right-hand drawer, in the back. Have James collect the pieces and see what you can do with them. And check eBay to see if you can find a replacement."

He slammed the phone down and gave Brandon a sour look. "You should have done that. It's not hard."

Brandon wiped at his eyes, and his voice shook. "I'm so sorry about all of this. About breaking it, and not speaking up. I feel awful."

Rick shrugged. "Things break. It's no big deal." He pursed his lips. "Are you happy living here?" *Poor kid, he's not used to having servants huddle about.*

Brandon's eyes widened. "God, yes. I'm so sorry. I only care about you. I want to make *you* glad I'm here." He sniffed. "Remember? You wanted someone to care for you. I'd like that to be me. Aren't *you* happy?"

"Me, happy?" His eye caught the portrait of Victoria on his desk, and his mind convulsed with the memory of the last time he'd seen her. Guilt clutched at his stomach as he muttered, "I think we'll just have to settle for you being happy." He pushed his chair back. "I'm afraid I'm pretty tired. Would you mind if I took a nap until Molly shows up?"

Brandon's lower lip trembled. "Can I lie with you?"

"Hmmph. Didn't you say you had homework or something to do? I'd really like to be alone for a bit, I think."

Brandon looked stricken, and Rick started to speak. But Victoria's cold eyes gazing at him from her photograph staunched his reply, and he strode from the room without another word.

Chapter Fourteen

"Good Golly Miss Molly"

Brandon sat behind the desk in Victoria's office, staring at nothing. His backpack rested on the polished wood, and his fingers flipped the straps idly back and forth. He blinked his puffy eyes and wiped at his nose, but his features remained stolid. Rick's face, impassive, almost cold, lingered in his mind. *He's not happy. What can I do, what can I do?* He jumped when the door opened.

James' apologetic tones did nothing to soothe his spirit. "I'm so sorry, sir. I didn't know you were here. I'll come back another time."

Brandon stared at him, recalling Rick's instructions about the figurine. "You're looking for the statue, aren't you?" He trundled the door open and shuffled amid the papers. "Here, where would you like the pieces?" Guilt twisted his heart as he arranged them in a neat row on the desk. "There's more than I remembered."

"I'll just take them, then, sir." James tried to gather them up, but the statuette had shattered into too many parts for him to hold in his hands.

"Here, use one of the boxes that held my books." Brandon reached into the well of the desk and pulled out a battered cardboard container.

"Thank you, sir."

Brandon made room while James swept the broken porcelain into the box. "I'm sorry to have caused so much trouble, James. I hope I can make it up to you."

"No trouble at all, sir. I'm here to help." He hesitated. "To be honest, I don't know why Daniels flew into such a rage over this. He's been erratic like that for more than a year now, not at all like himself. In any case, you know, I would have been glad to assist with your books, and then I would have been here to clean up for you when this trinket broke."

Brandon's face heated. "Thanks. I know you would have helped, but I didn't want to bother you."

"I enjoy helping, sir." He dropped his eyes. "It's really not my place to say so, sir, but I'm glad you're here. Mr. Collier has been so, well, *melancholy* since his wife departed. I thought I'd never see him smile again, to say nothing of standing up to Daniels like he just did. Miss Sandra has been happier, too. You seem to be a good influence on both of them, sir."

"Do you really think so, James?"

"Yes, sir." He hesitated. "I just wish Mrs. Collier was back. I'm sure they both miss her."

"I kind of had the impression that Sandra and her sister didn't get along?" Brandon thought the same about Rick and his wife, but decided against mentioning it.

"Well, they had their ups and downs, sir. When they were little girls, they were inseparable. They shared everything growing up, even boyfriends. After Victoria married

Mr. Collier, I was afraid they'd have a falling out, but they seemed to mend fences. Then, about a year ago, when Mr. Collier was out of town on business, things seemed to fall apart again. Mrs. Collier left before they had a chance to make up. It's so sad." His face colored and he murmured, "Perhaps I've spoken out of turn. I hope you're not offended."

"Not at all, James. I think a lot of both Rick and Sandra. I want them both to find happiness."

"As do I, sir. And if I may say so, it will be good for everyone to have a young person in the house again, to liven things up." His face crinkled into a smile. "If you need anything, please just let me know."

"I'll do that. Thank you, James. You've been so kind to me since I've been here."

"As have you to me, sir. Would you perhaps like some tea, or a soda? I'd be glad to bring you something."

"Gee, thanks. Really. But I guess what I'd like to do is get started on my homework. Maybe I'll stop by the kitchen later and you and Emma and I can have something?"

"We'd like that, sir. But don't hesitate to ask if you need anything." He departed with the pieces of the broken statue rattling in the box and left Brandon alone.

He pressed his palms into his eyes for a moment and heaved a deep breath. He pulled out his laptop, plugged it in, and powered it up. While he waited for Windows to load, his fingers poked through the pencil drawer in the desk. *I'll have to get some pens and notepads. I don't want to use* her *stationery.*

He ran nervous fingers along the underside of the drawer. They rubbed across something jammed between the desk and the runner. He dug at it and pulled out a secure digital card with 64GB displayed in bold, orange characters. *Wow. That would double the static memory on my tablet. Wonder how it got stuck up in there?* He slipped it into the slot on his machine and waited.

When the machine finished loading, he clicked on the memory card. *Only three gigabytes in use.* He opened it and saw a folder named Victoria's Documents, with the usual subfolders for My Videos, My Pictures, and My Music along with dozens of word processing files inside. Shrugging, he returned to the root directory and created a folder for Brandon's Documents. *There's still plenty of room for all my stuff. I'll just use this one for now and buy one of my own when I can afford it.*

He let a wan smile pass across his features as he thought about Rick's camera and the pictures and movies still inside of it, taken during their time together over the last two months. *Now that I've got room to store them on my computer, maybe I can make a DVD for us. It was almost like our honeymoon, after all.* Heartened by the memories of those pleasant days, Brandon used the browser to navigate to the web pages for Dr. LeClerc's course. He slipped out of Rick's shoes and flexed his toes in the plush carpet that covered the study's floor. Soon the world of experimental genetics consumed his mind.

Brandon stretched and looked away from his computer screen. Outside, the wind howled through the darkness and snow flickered in the glow from the lights in the landscaping. The ethereal illumination from his computer cast the only light in Victoria's study. He passed his mouse over the taskbar to check the time. *Jeez, it's almost seven.* He jammed his feet back into his shoes and decided to find something to eat. *Were we going to have dinner with Rick's sister? I don't remember. Emma will know.*

The chandeliers in the hallway cast a soft, golden hue over the corridor. He headed toward the front entry, intending to sneak through the Great Hall and into the kitchens, which were in the wing. The sound of voices from the parlor made him pause. He listened, thinking he should probably find Rick if his sister and her husband had arrived.

Daniels' precise syllables echoed against the hard surfaces and scratched at his ears. "Mr. Collier is resting, Mrs. Palmer. I can call him, if you wish."

"Oh, do let him sleep, Daniels." The woman's husky voice sounded as if it rasped against raw tissues in her throat. Brandon caught a whiff of cigarette smoke and wrinkled his nose. Her words continued to saw away at the air. "Tell me, is he still moping around over Victoria leaving him?"

"He seems a bit more *animated* since he returned from Chicago last week, ma'am."

"Oh yes, you called and warned me about that low-class scallion he brought home with him. I just can't believe he's let someone like that into Victoria's home."

"He seems quite taken with him, ma'am. They even have adjoining rooms."

Another voice, a man's, with a buzzsaw accent only an Iowan could love, broke in. "Now, Molly, you shouldn't be so judgmental. You know that Ricky's committed to that College. He's even on the Board of Regents. Maybe he's just helping a poor, needy student."

The woman's sniff echoed in the foyer. "Well, that doesn't mean he needs to turn his home into a dormitory. You know, he had more sense about these things until those Montgomery women got their talons in him. Speaking of talons, how is that sister-in-law of his? Still circling around, looking for a mouse to eat?"

Daniels' bland tones didn't indicate any objection to the characterization of Sandra. "She was here for Christmas, but she went back to Chicago. I'm not sure when she'll return to the Manor, ma'am."

"Good riddance. I don't think I could stand her snide remarks." Blue smoke drifted from the parlor and hung near the ceiling. Brandon could imagine her pausing for a puff or twenty before continuing. "What can you tell me about this Cinderfella he's moved in here, Daniels? I bet Ricky found him at a homeless shelter or some equally unseemly place. That would be just like him."

"I couldn't say, ma'am. But he seems to be quite muscular, almost like he worked as a dancer someplace."

"A dancer! You mean you think he was a male stripper? How perfectly obscene!"

Brandon suppressed a gasp when a hand gripped his shoulder. He whirled to see Rick standing behind him with a finger to his lips.

"Shh. Let's see how deep she digs herself," he whispered, grinning.

Daniels managed to fill his voice with disdain and professional detachment all at once. "The cleaning crew were gossiping about him this morning. I had to rebuke them about it. Mrs. Collier would never have tolerated such a houseguest. She was a saint, with all she had to put up with from her husband and her sister."

The man with the farmer's accent husked again. "Well, it seems to me that worked both ways. Her imitation of Lucretia Borgia could be pretty convincing."

Molly's laugh decayed into a fit of coughing before she responded. "Hah! I'd say the Montgomery clan was the *reincarnation* of the Borgias, except that's too mean to the Borgias!"

Rick leaned into Brandon and murmured, "I think we should make our appearance. Follow my lead." He swept into the room with Brandon in his wake. "Molly, how nice to see you!" He rushed up and pulled a plump, dark-haired woman to her feet by both her hands. They exchanged air kisses and a hug before he turned to the balding, corpulent fellow wallowing in a nearby overstuffed chair. "Rupert. Always a pleasure." They shook hands, but Rupert didn't stand and continued to lounge in his chair. Cigarettes moldered in ashtrays next to each of their seats.

"Daniels, thank you for entertaining my sister. Will you please tell Emma that we'll have dinner in, shall we say, fifteen minutes?"

"Yes, sir." Daniels scratched at the back of his hand, as though troubled by dry skin. He lurched to his feet and fussed with the ashtrays, dumping them into a trash can and making microscopic adjustments to the magazines stacked on the coffee table.

"Now, if you will, Daniels." Rick turned his back on him and tugged at Brandon's hand to bring him forward. Daniels scowled, but scuttled out of the room, still scratching.

"Molly, Rupert, I'd like you to meet our houseguest. This is Sandra's and my friend, Brandon. He won the Montgomery Fellowship at the College this spring, and he'll be staying at the Manor while he completes his studies."

Molly gave him the same flabby hugs and fake kisses that she'd exchanged with her brother. "So nice to meet you, Brannon." The scent of stale cigarette smoke and expensive perfume congealed about her like cheap barbecue sauce on prime rib.

Brandon's face heated. "That's Brandon, ma'am, not Brannon." He escaped by turning to Rupert to shake his hand. "Nice to meet you, too, sir."

The man's palm was slippery with sweat, and brown nicotine stains showed on his teeth when he smiled. He narrowed his eyes to slits, reminding Brandon of a pig burrowing for truffles. "So, you won a scholarship at school, eh? What will you study? Dance, maybe?"

"I'm pre-med, sir." Brandon gritted his teeth. This was going to be a long night.

Rick's eyes glinted. "He's got a position in our best research lab, in experimental genetics. They're working on enhancing canine intelligence, from what I understand." He turned to Brandon. "Maybe you should have a conversation with Rupert. He owns several hog farms in Iowa. Perhaps your research could improve porcine intelligence, too."

Rupert shook his head, and his chins waggled. "Pigs are too smart as it is. They're a lot like people, you know."

Rick's smile broadened. "So I hear. Speaking of pigs, how's the business holding up? Will you need another loan?"

Rupert turned a deep red at that. "Sales are down. This damned economy hurts everyone. And that blasted black socialist in the White House is gonna make it easier for unions to take over our meat processing plants. You mark my words, he's gonna ruin this country."

"Well, you know, I'd hate for the bank to have to call in your loan. But, as you say, things are tight all over."

"Now, now, Frederick. You wouldn't do that to your only sister, would you?" Molly wheezed and waggled her eyelashes at him. "We're so grateful for the help you've given us, you know. We'll never forget it."

"Nor will I, sis, nor will I."

She blinked at that and flopped back into her chair, which whooshed in response to the sudden weight. Her eyes narrowed as she spoke. "So, Frederick, tell me. Where is your delightful wife? Is she still off on her European adventure?"

Rick paled a bit at that, and Brandon shuddered. *God, I feel sorry for any kids these people have. Come to think of it, they'd probably eat their young anyway. How did Rick turn out the way he did, having this person for a sister?*

Rick's voice was steady. "Victoria hasn't returned yet."

"I'm so *sorry*, Ricky!" She lit a new cigarette from the stub in her ashtray and snuffed out the old one. A cloud of noxious blue smoke leaked out from her nose and lips. "You must be so lonely. I mean, a man has *needs*, physical needs."

Rupert harrumphed. "Maybe he's not like most men, Molly. When we were in high school, he never sniffed around poontang like the other guys. He was always focused on his studies. I bet he's drowned himself in work at the bank." He lit another cigarette. "Am I right, Ricky?"

"The bank has kept me busy, especially with the financial emergency." Rick's jaws jumped, and he avoided Brandon's eyes.

Molly snorted. "Nonsense, Rupert. All men are pigs. I should know." A sly smile played with her lips as her eyes raked over Brandon before turning back to her brother. "How ever do you manage, my dear?"

"I manage fine, not that it's any of your business." A chime sounded. "Ah, that will be Emma telling us dinner is ready. Shall we go?"

As the others left for the dining room, Rick grabbed Brandon by the elbow and steered him to one side. "I promise you this will be over soon, and they'll head back to Des Moines. If you want to eat in the kitchen with Emma, feel free and I'll make excuses," he whispered.

"I'll stand by my man. Should I sing it for them?" Brandon whispered back.

Rick chuckled. "That might be a bit much. They're harmless enough, and there's no real reason to offend them or fight with them. You sure you don't want to leave?"

"No. Unless you want me to?" *It's like he's trying to get rid of me. Is he ashamed of me? Or our relationship?*

Rick shrugged. "It's your funeral. I bet Emma prepared pork roast, in honor of Rupert."

Chapter Fifteen

"Who Wants to Live Forever?"

Rick counted down the seconds to midnight and popped a fresh bottle of champagne when the New Year began. "Who needs more bubbly?"

"I do!" Brandon reached for Sandra's glass. "Permit me, my lady. I'll serve you!"

"That's sweet, but why don't you put another log on the fire? Then we can toast the New Year and toss our glasses into the flames."

"That works!" Brandon leaped to tend to the fire.

Rick waited until everyone had their glasses and raised his in a toast. "I should say something fancy, but the best I can come up with is, to us!"

"Hear, hear!" Brandon drained his champagne flute and held it out. "More. I could develop a taste for this stuff."

Rick grinned and poured him another glass. "And you told me you thought it tasted like carbonated vinegar."

Sandra giggled. "That was when he was still sober. I'll have some too."

A dull rumble thudded through the air, and a light flashed in the distance. Brandon frowned and gazed out the window. "What was that?"

Rick shrugged. "Probably just some locals setting off fireworks. It's a New Year's tradition hereabouts."

"Really? I thought fireworks were illegal?"

Sandra smiled at him. "You silly boy. That's what I love about you. You're so innocent. What's your opinion about the tooth fairy?"

"If he's a fairy, he can't be all bad." Brandon flipped through the DVDs. "Are we going to watch *It's a Wonderful Life* tonight?"

"Only if you want to see me hurl." Sandra looked at the selection. "Hey, you've got season four of *CSI*. How about that? I love that show!"

"Sure, why not?" Brandon loaded it into the machine while Rick lounged back on the sofa and Sandra settled into a nearby easy chair. He cuddled next to Brandon and relaxed. Even though Greg Sanders reminded him of Brandon, he floated between watching and sleep. When his cell phone shrilled, he jumped. "Who could be calling at this hour, on New Year's Eve?" He flipped it open and walked across the room so as to not disturb the others.

When he returned, he collapsed into a chair and dropped his phone on the coffee table with a clatter. The flickering warmth from the fireplace did nothing to warm the chill that froze his heart.

"Rick, what's wrong?" Brandon knelt at his feet and grasped his hand. "You look like you've seen a ghost."

"Those fireworks we heard. It was kids messing around at the carriage house, and it caught on fire. That was Sam Sondergard, calling to let me know." Rick closed his eyes. He couldn't look at Brandon.

Sandra tossed her head. "It needed to be torn down. I don't know why you didn't do it after Victoria fired the contractors last spring. It was nothing but a hazard anyway, half-remodeled like she left it."

Rick shook his head. "A hazard. Yes, I was worried about that." He shuddered.

Brandon peered at him. "Can I get you anything? More champagne, maybe?"

"No. It hardly seems right to celebrate, in view of what the firemen found down there."

Sandra's eyes narrowed at that, and her face paled. "What did they find?"

"According to Sam, the firemen found a body."

Brandon gasped. "A body! That's awful! Is it someone we know? Are the kids okay?"

Rick stared at him without emotion. "Sam didn't say if they'd identified it, but I'm pretty sure I know who it is."

"Who?" Brandon tightened his grip on Rick's hands.

"And how would you know?" Sandra asked, her voice a low murmur, as if she were speaking to herself.

"It's got to be Victoria." Rick's voice shook. "It can't be anyone else."

"But she's in Europe! Studying art. You said so!" Brandon rapped out the words, and they beat against his conscience.

"It's a long story." He sighed and stared into the fire. Silence stretched.

Sandra stood and gripped his shoulder. "Well, I think you should tell us everything,

Rick." She glanced at Brandon. "Whatever it is, we'll stand by you. Won't we, Brandon?"

"Of course. You can count on us, Rick."

He pursed his lips and looked at them. "You don't know that. You can't know that."

Sandra sat in the chair opposite him. The flames from the fireplace cast a ruddy glow on her hair, and her eyes were deep pools of concern. "Just tell us what happened, Rick. It can't be as bad as you seem to think."

He heaved a sigh and stared at the floor by Brandon's knees. "It all happened last March." The memories of that day had lain coiled in his soul, gnawing at him for nearly a year. "Did you know that Victoria had affairs during our marriage? From the first week we were married, in fact."

Sandra snorted. "Rick, honey, if that's the big news, it won't stop any presses. No one said anything to you out of deference to your feelings. But we all knew."

He glanced at her. It was as though she spoke from another planet. "Did you know she slept with Daniels?"

She shook her head. "I suspected, but wasn't sure. He got so supercilious the last few months before she vanished, I thought something was up."

"Well, she did. I'd caught him sneaking out of her room the week before. At first, I was so shocked I let it be, but I then decided I had to confront her about it. I mean, I knew she wasn't faithful. But doing it in our home, and with an employee! That was too much."

"Really? You stood up to her? Good for you!" Sandra's eyes flashed.

Brandon sat in silence, his eyes wide and his face a frozen mask.

"She just laughed at me. She said she'd sleep with anyone she wanted anywhere she wanted, and there wasn't anything I could do about it."

"I hope you reminded her that's grounds for divorce, and that your pre-nup guaranteed you a fat settlement if she was unfaithful."

Brandon's tenor piped into the conversation. "Rick, what's this got to do with the body the firemen found?"

"I'm getting to that." He stared at his lover. "I've a confession for you, too. Back then, before I met you, I'd arrange business trips every month or so and go to baths and sex clubs. I've been with dozens of men before you."

Brandon's face turned a deep red. "Who cares who you were with before we met? Not me, that's who!"

Rick shook his head. "Well, I was unfaithful to Victoria. And she knew about it. She'd hired a private detective, and he'd taken pictures and movies of me. She showed me on her cell phone."

Sandra *tsk*ed. "Poor Rick. That's so like Victoria. I suppose she planned some kind of blackmail?"

"That's it. She said it was convenient for her to have a show husband. That's what she called me. She said I could sleep around all I wanted, as long as I was discreet, but she demanded the same privilege. She laughed at me and told me she'd had dozens of lovers. She said I was only good for cover, so she could have affairs without any scandal. She even said her current lover was someone I knew, that he was richer than I'd ever be. She told me she was going to fly to Switzerland and have his baby, and I'd have to put up with it and pretend it was mine. I balked, but she said she'd show the pictures to the Board at the bank, and to our customers, that she'd ruin me if I didn't do what she said."

Sandra's eyes snapped in firelight. "The bitch. So you told her to piss off, right?"

"I didn't know what to do. It was all so *unexpected*. I mean, I knew we weren't happy, and if I'd thought about it I would have realized how bad it was between us. But, I mean, the marriage seemed convenient to me, too. It was like I had two lives—the real one, with Victoria, and then this other life where I had sex with men."

Brandon nodded. "And when she showed you the pictures, you knew that no one has two lives. You had one life that you put into two compartments, and now she dumped them together. You were confused and didn't know what to do." He paused, and his eyes bored into Rick. "What did you do?"

"I got drunk, that's what I did. While we were fighting, she got a call from that damned contractor she'd hired for the carriage house. She cussed him out and said he was fired. She stalked out of the room and told me she was going to kick him off the property."

Brandon nodded. "So, that was the last time you saw her?"

Rick's breath shuddered in his chest. "No. I saw her once more after that."

"Tell us," Brandon whispered. Sandra sat across from them, in silence, her face pale.

"I thought about what had happened, about our fight, for an hour or more, and then I decided to try to reason with her. She was going to make me her slave. I couldn't live like that! I planned to throw myself on her mercy, plead with her to just let me disappear." He stopped.

"Go on. Let it all out." Brandon squeezed his hand.

"So...I looked for her in the Manor, but she wasn't around. I walked down to the carriage house. It was nearly sunset, but there was still enough light to see. I called out, but no one answered. The door to the old coal cellar was open, so I went down there. That was where I found her."

"Go on, tell us what happened then. It'll be all right." Brandon's voice urged him on, like a priest at a confessional.

"Nothing happened. I mean, I found her. She was lying there next to the pile of coal, not moving, and there was blood pooled under head. I remember the smell and the color. It was so dark, more like wine than blood. I checked for a pulse, and couldn't find one. I didn't know what to do. Daniels had heard us fighting, and I was sure I'd be accused of her murder."

"But she was dead when you found her?"

"I thought so. That must be right, if they found a body there tonight."

"So, after you found her, what did you do?" Brandon's voice was stronger now, more certain.

"Well, I remember thinking my life was over. My marriage was a disaster, now my wife was dead, and I was going to be charged with murder. Everyone would know about my other life, with men, and I'd be humiliated. You know, she told me that she'd hidden copies of those pictures where I'd never find them. I rifled through her desk, and even searched the carriage house, but she was right. They were nowhere."

"You didn't call the police, or tell anyone?"

"Why bother? I figured the police would come soon enough and arrest me. I'd been drinking, did I say that? I came back up here and I...I took some sleeping pills. I wasn't really trying to kill myself, but it was in my head. I didn't wake up until late the next afternoon."

"You tried to hurt yourself. That's what you were thinking about when I found you in Secret Canyon, wasn't it? You were going to jump and kill yourself." Brandon's soft voice held no accusation, only compassion.

"I guess. I was thinking about how screwed up I was, am. James, bless his heart, must have suspected. He woke me up every couple hours that night. I cussed him out at the time." A shaky grin tugged at his lips. "But you're the one who really saved me, Brandon. You brought my life back into focus and gave me hope." He glanced out the window in the direction of the carriage house. "But now no one can save me. It'll all come out, just like I feared. And you'll be mixed up in it. I should have never brought you here. I'm sorry." He glanced at Sandra and looked away. "I've betrayed you, too. I'm worthless."

Sandra's firm voice carried comfort and assurance. "Don't ever say that. You mean too much to too many people. Like me. And Brandon."

Brandon's pure tenor sang out. "That's right. You didn't really do anything wrong. After all, she was already dead. What difference could it have made if you'd called the police?"

"Well, I was sure the scandal about me being gay would come out, and no one would believe me that I didn't kill her. Between that and her affairs, I had plenty of motive, and it happened on the estate. That's opportunity. What else do they need? I was sure I'd go to prison for a murder I didn't commit." He stopped and licked his lips. "But then, later, I decided maybe she wasn't dead after all."

Sandra frowned. "I don't understand. You said she had no pulse, and she was lying there in a pool of blood?"

"No pulse I could feel, at least. But when I checked the cellar the next day, she was gone! The place was all cleaned up. No body, no blood, nothing. Just a dusty pile of coal."

"That just means the real murderer came back and hid the body." Sandra shook her head. "You should have called the police then, for sure."

"Maybe. But by then I wasn't sure she was really dead. See, there's the missing money to consider. You called me about it the next day, after I woke up. Remember?"

"*That's* when this all happened? I sure do remember! But the money got moved at seven that morning. If she was dead the night before, she couldn't have been in Chicago the next morning to do the transfer."

"Exactly."

Sandra's fingers drummed on the end table. She jumped to her feet and paced back and forth. "By the time I called you, we knew the money was gone, that the transfers had been done on Victoria's computer at the bank, and whoever did it used her passwords and her accounts."

"I know! And the body was gone from the carriage house. I mean, she'd *told* me she was going to run off to Switzerland, and you were so *sure* she'd taken the money. I wondered if I'd imagined it all, or if maybe she was just knocked out. Later, when Sam only found her fingerprints on her computer at the bank, I thought for sure she must have just been unconscious, woken up, and gone to Chicago to get the money."

"The fingerprint evidence wasn't exactly conclusive. They just didn't find anyone else's prints on her keyboard or in her office." Sandra pursed her lips. "So that was where the idea for the cover story about her going to Europe came from? What she told you when the two of you fought?"

"I guess it must have. Actually, I thought that was your idea. Whatever, it fit with what I knew."

"You don't have any idea who this Swiss lover is?"

"No. I don't think he was Swiss, though. I had the impression he's someone we knew, in Chicago."

"What about the pictures? You said they were on her cell phone?" Sandra was all business, gathering data like a police investigator.

Pent-up anxiety drained from Rick with her questioning, letting it all come out. "Her cell phone was in pieces on the floor of the coal cellar when I found her. It was like someone stomped on it. When I went back the next day, it was gone, too."

Brandon shook his head. "I don't care what happened. I'm just glad you didn't do anything wrong, Rick. But I'll stand by you, no matter what!"

Rick's cell phone shrilled again. He glanced at it. "It's the undersheriff. I can't talk to him."

Sandra snatched up the phone. "Hello." She listened and nodded. "This is Sandra. He's indisposed." She nodded. "Uh-huh." Another long pause. "I understand." Pause. "Thank you, Sam. I appreciate your sympathies. I'll give your condolences to Rick." She flipped the phone closed and put her hands on her hips. "Well, they've already identified Victoria's body. He says it looks like she's only been dead a few days from the condition of the remains."

"What? So then she *was* just knocked out when I saw her last March?" Confusion flooded through Rick at the news.

"Could be. But Sam says there's two bodies, and there's something strange about both of them. He wants to wait for the coroner's report."

Rick jumped and his heart stopped. "What did you say? Bodies? Plural?"

"Yeah, that's what the man said. Victoria and a John Doe, both buried under the coal in the old cellar."

Chapter Sixteen

"Another One Bites the Dust"

Brandon eased his car into the lot next to the zoology labs and parked next to Dr. LeClerc's muddy jeep. He splashed through icy puddles of slush and made his way to the red brick, Gothic-style building. The terrazzo floor of the entryway gleamed in the sunlight before it disappeared into the shadows of empty hallways. He hesitated, and then strolled through the building toward Allen's lab, his footfalls echoing on the hard surfaces. On each side, glass walls opened into labs filled with equipment and experiments, waiting for the students and researchers to return from the holiday break.

The door to the Canine Genomics Facility stood open, and bright fluorescent lighting pooled in the hallway. He stopped and rapped at the glass. "Dr. LeClerc? Is anyone here?" In one corner, coffee dripped into a half-filled pot. *Someone must be here, since there's coffee brewing.* He stepped inside and looked over the gleaming test tubes and the controls for the electron microscopes. Desks for the student assistants were interspersed between the immaculate lab benches. Brandon's lips turned down at the disarray he saw on most of the student spaces, and he resolved to keep his area as neat as Dr. LeClerc's.

"Who's there?" Allen bustled from the back of the room, wiping his hands on his white lab coat. "Brandon? Is that you?"

"Yeah. I hope it's okay that I came in today. I kind of needed to get out of the house for a while."

Allen nodded his head. "Sure. Classes don't start for another couple weeks, though, so there's not much of anyone around. I think the bookstore and registrar might be open, though."

"Yeah, the parking lot was pretty empty. I guess I can get enrolled and maybe pick up my books. Do you know if the financial aid office is open?"

"Got me. I think it's upstairs from the registrar, though, so you can check it out when you go over there."

"Thanks." Brandon looked around the lab. "You need help with anything today?"

"No, thanks. There's not much going on, I'm afraid." He grinned. "Tell you what, though. I could use a break. You want some coffee, and we could chat a bit?"

"Sure. I'd like that."

Allen rinsed out two mismatched mugs and poured for both of them. He dumped a generous helping of sugar into his and stirred it while he settled onto a lab stool. "I was just working on a paper for *Biochimica.* I hate writing. The fun part of research is doing it."

"I feel the same way. I like doing lab work, but writing up the reports and turning them in is drudgery."

"Necessary drudgery, though. Sam says his work is the same. Investigating crimes is the fun part, where he gets to solve a puzzle. But the paperwork is every policeman's bane."

Brandon pulled out a chair and stacked the papers from the seat onto a desktop. "I guess he's got quite a case to work on now. A double murder." He shuddered and sipped at his coffee. His chair creaked when he settled into it and lounged back.

"Yeah. It's a real puzzler, too. How's Rick holding up? It must have been a shock to him."

"It sure was. We were watching a DVD when Sam first called with the news. We didn't know what to think. And then he called back, and one of the dead bodies turned out to be Rick's wife!"

"Sam's having fits over this whole thing. You know that he investigated Victoria's disappearance last spring?"

Brandon nodded. "Sandra mentioned that last week. Rick filled in more details last night, after we found out whose body it was. Something about some missing money at the bank?"

"Yeah. It all looked so plausible then, that she'd just run off with a lover to avoid paying Rick alimony. The poor guy. But now it turns out she was dead all along."

"What? I thought that Sam said she couldn't have been dead very long, based on the condition of the body?"

"Now, that's the fascinating part, from a biological perspective." Allen pursed his lips, and his eyes lit up. "I guess I can discuss what Allen told me. After all, there'll be a coroner's inquest where the details will all come out, so it won't be telling tales out of school. It seems that the bodies were, uh, disinfected, so to speak."

Brandon shook his head. "Huh? I mean, excuse me?"

"Well, look, you know that the coroner can usually say something about time of death based on the condition of the cadaver, right? Temperature and rigor are clues if they find the body soon enough. Later the state of decomp, and the insects that are feeding on the corpse, give another, less accurate timeline."

"Sure. Like on *CSI*."

"Yeah. Except that those markers are all screwed up in this case. In the first place, the corpses were both in airtight body bags, like they use in a morgue, or on a battlefield."

"Body bags! You mean the *killer* put them in body bags? Why would he do that?"

"That's the puzzle. But there's method to his madness. First, there're no insects, since they were sealed up. Even if the bags hadn't been airtight, someone filled them with pesticides after the bodies were put in."

"Pesticides? I don't get it. That makes no sense at all."

Allen grinned. "It's a biological problem, so I'll leave it as an exercise for the student. You tell me." He sipped some coffee and leaned back, waiting for Brandon to figure it out.

"Well...I guess the pesticides would kill the beetles and maggots that ordinarily feed on a decomposing body?"

"Exactly. Except that they were already sealed out by the bag. What else?"

"They're toxic chemicals. So if the...*bodies* weren't already dead, the pesticides would have killed them, being sealed up in the airtight bags."

"It's pretty clear they were already dead. A broken neck in her case, and a bullet in the brain in his, seem to have taken care of that. But from a forensic point of view, the chemicals have messed up the decomp timeline. It would appear that they were absorbed through the skin and killed off the bodies' own internal bacteria."

"You're kidding! I didn't know such a thing was possible. So, airtight bags, no bugs, and no bacteria. That means the bodies didn't decay at all. Kind of like they were embalmed, without being embalmed. Am I right?"

"Exactly. Go to the head of the class. And no stink, either. It's like they've been disinfected and then put in a sealed environment. There was no decomp at all. Even with bodies sealed in airtight bags, you'd expect all the soft tissues to turn to soup after the internal bacteria get to work. But that didn't happen here because the pesticides killed the internal bacteria. So at first the coroner thought they'd been dead just a week or two. But now, he doesn't have a clue. They could have been dead for two weeks or as much as nine months."

"Why nine months?"

"That's the last time anyone saw Mrs. Collier alive, last March sometime. Sam's got the exact date. That's when she fired some contractors at the estate who were renovating the carriage house."

"So, what does Sam think? The murderer must have known that the combination of body bags and pesticide would mess up the time of death?"

"Maybe. Sam said he thought the idea might have been to just keep the corpses from smelling. A decomposing body stinks to high heaven, and if the murderer wanted to hide the bodies, this would have been a good strategy."

"How could anyone have known that would work?"

"I guess this kind of thing happened at least once before. Sam said he read a paper on it by some guy in Tennessee at the body farm there."

"Ugh. Body farm?"

"Yeah. Sam went there to study one summer. They get bodies donated to them, like a medical school, you know? But they use them to train people in forensic pathology. Anyway, there's a similar case that this one researcher wrote up."

"Still, that's pretty specialized knowledge. That should help narrow down the suspects, right?"

"Turns out, the answer's no. There was a *CSI* episode a couple of years back where the murderer used the same trick. Anyone who's a fan of the show could have figured this out."

"Jeez. It's still pretty gruesome. What kind of monster would stuff a corpse in a body bag and fill it with insecticide?"

"Sam says you'd be surprised what normal people will do. Didn't you study the Milgram experiments in your psych classes?"

"You mean the behavioral experiments back in the sixties?" Brandon frowned. "Let's see. A group of subjects were told to administer electrical shocks to actors, right? As I recall, there weren't any real shocks, but the actors screamed like they were really being tortured. Most people just followed orders and kept on pushing the button. We studied it as an example of unethical research."

"Yeah. Most people went ahead and did it, even when they thought it might kill the person supposedly getting shocked. It was unethical for sure, even though no one was really hurt, since there was no informed consent from the subjects. Some of them had psych problems afterwards, too. But it sure proved that ordinary people will do horrible things under the right circumstances."

"I guess." Brandon shook his head. "Hey, how about the body bags? I wouldn't even know where to get one. Isn't that a clue? Couldn't they trace them or something?"

"Dunno. It's not like they're a controlled substance or anything. I'm sure Sam's checking on it. He'll figure it out. He always does."

"You two have been together for a while, haven't you?"

"Yeah. He's pretty special. I don't know what I'd do without him."

"I feel the same way about Rick."

Allen raised his eyebrows. "You know, Sam and I have wondered about Rick. Not to speak ill of the dead, but it was never clear to us why he put up with that woman he was married to. So you two are really a couple? Good for you! It's all right if you don't want to talk about it. But I promise you I won't tell anyone, either."

Brandon blushed. "I hope we're a couple. I thought we were. It's kind of strange.

Sometimes he acts like we are, and sometimes he seems to want to hide it. I think he's worried about what people at the bank might think. I just want him to be happy." Brandon hated the way his voice trembled at the last word.

"You know, it's tough coming out, especially for someone in his position. You can talk to me anytime. I'll respect his privacy, and yours too."

"I appreciate that. I feel so isolated since coming to the Manor, and he's been so different. Distracted, even cold sometimes. When his sister and her husband visited, I could have sworn he wanted to get rid of me."

"Is he out to them?"

"I don't think he's out to anyone, even himself. Don't get me wrong, we've slept together every night since our first time, and the sex is fantastic." Brandon's face heated, but he went on. "It's still like he's got two lives. One in private, where we're lovers, then one with everyone else, where I'm a protégé or guest or something."

Allen frowned. "You know, it must be hard for him. It sounds like he's still coming to terms with being gay. When I was in college, I volunteered at a help line, and I saw a lot of this. It would be good for both of you to have someone to talk to." He drummed his fingers on the lab bench. "Tell you what. Let me give you my cell phone number. Next time you're feeling isolated, or just need someone to talk to, call me." He scribbled on a business card and thrust it into Brandon's hands. "I mean it, now. Put me on speed dial on your phone."

Brandon took the card and stuffed it in his shirt pocket. A shaky smile trembled on his lips. "Thanks, I'll do that. I appreciate it, really."

"It's not just for you. It'll help Rick, too, if you've got someone else to talk to. We owe him a lot. We wouldn't be at Montgomery College if it weren't for him and Sandra."

"He's great. I'm so grateful for the opportunities he's given me."

"Just remember, a relationship is a two-way street. You do things for him, too. That's how it works with Sam and me, and *he* saved my life, so I owe him big time."

"I feel the same way about Rick—like he's saved my life."

"In our case, Sam literally saved my life. Back in Oregon, there was this psycho serial killer who kidnapped gay guys off the campus and murdered them. He'd troll around and sucker young men into the back of his van, kind of like in *Silence of the Lambs*. I wasn't careful and he got me. Sam blew his brains out as he was about to slit my throat."

"Wow. Rick said he'd solved some big case out west. You're pretty lucky."

"Sure am. It was luck that brought us here, too, where there were jobs for both of us. I had post-doc offers from Johns Hopkins and Rice, but there was nothing for Sam. Rick and Sandra were on the hiring committee that interviewed me, and they pulled strings to get him the undersheriff job."

"They're pretty special, all right. I love that she hangs out with us, but she seems kind of lonely sometimes."

"I think she's been down for the last year or so. First she broke up with that rich guy she was dating, and then her sister disappeared. She didn't really perk up until you came around. You seem to have that effect on people." He gulped the last of his coffee. "Want some more?"

"Sure. I'll get it." While he filled the cups, Brandon mused, "I didn't know she'd been dating someone. Was it serious?"

"I thought so. He was a houseguest for a week or so at the Manor two summers ago. As I recall, Rick was gone someplace, but she and this guy took me out to lunch. He was nice. A wicked sense of humor, and good looking if you like short, wiry guys, sort of like a gymnast. He ran some big bank or something in Chicago."

"So what happened between them?"

"I'm not sure. Later that year, in the fall, he was at a fundraiser for the College and spent all of his time sucking up to Victoria. That was strange all by itself, since she almost never came to College events. She was more into art galleries and that church in the village." Allen shook his head. "Poor Rick. She was always flirting and rubbing his nose in it." Allen sighed. "How did the two of you meet?"

"It was kind of strange, really. We first met last July at an art gallery, and then again the next week, by chance, on a tour in Sedona. Our paths didn't cross again until we ran into each other in Chicago, right after the election. I'd just ended a painful relationship, and Rick seemed so nice, and he was alone, too. It was like perfect timing for both of us. When I got the scholarship here, he suggested I stay at the Manor."

"Sounds like a match made in heaven." Allen slurped at his coffee.

"I thought so. Until two nights ago, at least. Everyone's pretty shaken up right now."

"I guess murder can do that. Don't worry. Sam will figure it all out. And don't forget, one way or another, things always work out. It might not be the way you expect, but things *always* work out."

Chapter Seventeen

"Love Me Tender"

Rick paced back and forth in his study, hands clasped behind his back and his eyes downcast. He squinted against the afternoon sun that slanted through the windows and reflected off the polished surface of his desk. One of Victoria's despised paintings, an abstract splash of blacks, maroons, and forest greens, nagged at him from where it hung on one wall. From the other wall a portrait of Phineas, her father, scowled at him.

Sandra's eyes tracked back and forth, watching him. "I wish you'd sit down. I can't think with you stomping around like that." She sat at attention on the sofa in front of the fireplace. Brandon looked on in silence from a chair hidden in one corner.

"I've got every reason to stomp around. My wife's dead. I conspired to cover up her disappearance. Sondergard already knows that. How long do you think it'll take him to discover she'd hired a PI and that she had dirt on me? How long do you think before he shows up to arrest me?"

"It doesn't have to work that way. Victoria treated lots of people like dirt. Any one of them could have done it. Maybe the contractor offed her because she fired him."

"Right. How about the other body? We don't even know who *that* is! Maybe it's the PI she hired to spy on me. Wouldn't that be just great?"

She sighed. "Just relax, will you? Don't borrow trouble. You tell him, Brandon."

"It'll work out, Rick. I know it will. You didn't do anything wrong. Allen says Sam always figures these things out."

"That's what I'm afraid of," he muttered. The phone rang and Rick turned to his desk, where he glanced at the caller ID. "It's the bank. What could they want?" He pressed the speakerphone and barked, "Yes?"

He recognized Mark Perkins, his staff assistant. "Mr. Collier, I'm so sorry to bother you. Please accept my sincerest condolences on your loss."

Rick's features softened. "Thanks, Mark. You'll understand we're all pretty upset here. I'm sorry I was short with you. What do you need?"

"Sir, that Sheriff person is back here. The one who investigated last March, when Mrs. Collier first disappeared."

"Sam Sondergard. Of course, he's probably investigating my wife's death. Give him anything he asks for."

"Yes sir, I will. He said to make it legal, he'd have to record your permission."

Rick's chair swooshed when he sat in it. "Of course. Put him on."

"Rick, this is Sam. I'm sorry to have to bother you."

"Not at all, Sam. You're doing your job. I want this over as much as anyone. What do I need to do?"

"We'd like to search Victoria's office at the bank. We never did find her appointment calendar last March, and I'd like to turn her computer over to a team of forensic specialists."

As those words piped from the phone's speaker, Brandon gave a little start.

Sam continued, "I'd also like to look at your appointment calendar. I'm officially asking for your consent to conduct a search. I don't have a warrant, and you have the right to refuse. I'm going to record your answer."

"You have my consent to search. Go ahead. I already told Mark to give you full cooperation." Rick paused and licked his lips. "Sam?"

"Yes, Mr. Collier?"

"Follow this wherever it takes you, all right?"

"I always do, sir."

"Of course. I know it doesn't matter for what you have to do, but I didn't kill her."

"No reason to think you did, sir. We're just starting our investigation, and this will help us rule you out."

"Right. Do you know who the other victim was?"

"We traced him through his fingerprints. Turns out they were on file with the SEC. He was one Brian Steadman, CEO of Axinon Investments. Seems the U.S. Attorney and the FBI have been looking for him."

A little gasp escaped from Sandra's mouth, and her hand went to her lips.

"Steadman, huh? I sort of knew him, and I think he and Sandra might have served on some boards together a couple of years ago.

Any idea how he wound up dead in my carriage house?"

"Not yet, sir. Don't worry, we'll figure it all out."

"I'm sure you will, Sam." The phone went dead and he stared at the others. "Jesus H. Christ. How the hell is Steadman tied to this?"

Sandra shook her head, and her voice trembled. "It just gets deeper and deeper, doesn't it?"

Rick peered at her. "I'm sorry. Didn't the two of you date for a while a couple of years ago?"

She passed her hands over her eyes, as if banishing some dreadful memory from her sight. "Yes. For a time there, I thought he might be the one. But...it didn't work out."

"I'm sorry you had to hear about it this way. It can't be easy, even if you weren't close anymore. You dated him, what, two summers ago, as I recall. I was off attending to that merger in Dallas, but I remember Victoria saying something about it."

She scowled and her eyes snapped. "Victoria. Right. She always noticed who I was dating." She shrugged. "It turned out I was interested in a relationship and he was interested in...well, let's just say it turned out we weren't as compatible as I thought. His tastes were a bit unseemly."

"His tastes?"

"I'd rather not talk about it." Her head gave a prim nod, and her eyes glittered.

"Uh, Rick?" Brandon's voice was soft and hesitant, almost as if he were unwilling to break in.

Rick lifted his eyebrows. Brandon had been so quiet that he'd forgotten he was there. "What is it? I'm sorry you have to go through all this."

"Sam, I mean the undersheriff; he mentioned he couldn't find Mrs. Collier's address book. Uh, I think I might know where it's at."

Rick shook his head. "How could you possibly know that?"

Brandon fidgeted in his seat. "A couple of days ago I was fiddling with her desk, kind of poking around. I didn't mean to snoop or anything, really! But I found this SD card jammed underneath one of the drawer glides. It had tons of spare space on it, so I stuck it into my tablet. I figured I'd put it back when I could afford to buy my own memory card."

Sandra's voice was like honey. "Baby, you should have said something. Your Aunt Sandra will buy you as many of those memory thingees as you need."

Brandon flushed. "Thanks, but I didn't think it would hurt anything. It had a windows folder named 'Victoria's Documents,' you know, like on your PC. I didn't look at her files. I just made my own directory."

Rick nodded. "Well, go get it and we'll check it out. This might break the case." He reached for the phone.

Sandra held up her hand. "Rick, wait. Who are you calling?"

"Sam, of course. He said he needed to find her calendar."

"Think, Rick. It sounds like she'd squirreled this away in her desk. You said she had hidden those pictures she was going to blackmail you with. Maybe they're on that memory thing he found. Don't you think we should at least see what's there first?"

Rick frowned. "We can't conceal any evidence from the authorities. It'll just make me look worse. If I'm the one turning this over to them, won't that be worth something?"

"Not if it's incriminating. Brandon, be a dear and bring your computer here. I want to look at those files. If it bothers the delicate sensibilities of you men, just leave the room."

Rick nodded to him. "Brandon, it's all right. Bring the card here, and we'll put it into my computer." He pressed the power button on his system and watched the younger man rush out of the room.

He stared at the computer screen and murmured, "What do you suppose we'll find?"

She shook her head. "Who knows? Maybe we'll hit the jackpot and crack the case." She pulled one of the visitor chairs behind the desk and sat where she could see the screen.

Brandon huffed back into the room and handed over the chip. He stood behind Rick and put his hands on his lover's shoulders. "You're so tense."

Rick twisted away. "I have a right to be tense." He hesitated, flipping the card in his fingers. "I still don't feel quite right about this. I think we should just call Sam."

"Oh, don't be such a weenie. Give me that thing!" She snatched it from him, stood, and slipped it into the slot on his computer. She pushed him aside and clicked with his mouse to browse through the files. "There's a bunch of documents. Let's see." She scrolled through the names. "I see her appointment file." She clicked it open and scanned through it. "What's this? Corydon Women's Health Center, Rock Island. Why would she go to a clinic in Rock Island? She and I both use Madeleine List in Chicago for our OBGYN doctor. She's the best there is."

Rick shook his head. "Another mystery."

She shrugged and scrolled on down. "I don't see any detective agencies listed." She frowned. "Let me check out the pictures and video folders. If she hid those photos there, we can delete them. One less thing to worry about."

Brandon touched her arm. "Sandra, I don't think that's a good idea."

"What? You want Rick should go to jail?"

"Of course not, but suppose there's another copy of this? Plus, I think they can tell when it got changed and recover the older versions. They do that on *CSI* all the time. They'll figure out that we tried to cover this up."

She scowled at him. "You might be right." Her gaze returned to the computer. "Still, we at least need to see what's here." The cursor raced across the screen. "The photo album's empty. Oh, something's in the video folder. Damn, there's just one file." Disappointment showed in her voice as she clicked on it.

The screen flickered and a new window opened, revealing a grainy home video file. The camera panned across a room filled with shadows and the glimmer of steel. Rick's lips dragged down on his face. "It looks like an S&M dungeon. The walls are painted black and the windows are blocked off. Look, there's chains attached to that bed. Are those plastic sheets? God, what's that shit hanging from those racks?"

"I see whips, and tit clamps," Brandon whispered. "There's handcuffs, and gags, and that's a male chastity belt. Those are butt plugs." His fingers pointed to a shelf near the window. "That can't be a gun on that chest, can it?"

"It sure looks like it. Hey, what's that thing?" Sandra pointed to a bar with padded shackles welded to the ends.

"It's a spreader bar. The cuffs go around the sub's ankles." Brandon pointed to a similar device with a round hoop welded in the middle. "That one is for the arms, and that collar in the middle goes around the sub's neck. See the padlocks?"

Rick looked at him and felt like he was seeing a stranger. "I wouldn't have any idea what this crap is for. How come you know so much about it?"

"I never told you. Peter was way into this stuff. His basement was full of it. I was his sub. You must have noticed the chain I was wearing around my neck in Sedona."

"You mean that bicycle chain? I thought it was just some peculiar jewelry kids wore nowadays. I didn't think about it, and you never wore it after we got together."

"It was a way of saying to the public I was his Boy. I was proud of it, then. It seems so foolish now that I'm with you."

The window flickered again, and the scene changed. Rick gaped. "Is that a body bag on the bed? With a *body* in it?"

"Yeah. This is really extreme, more than Peter and I ever did. See that tube coming out of it, with the duct tape around the base? That's so the sub can breathe. This is another kind of restraint. I guess this tells us where the murderer must have gotten the body bags used at the crime scene."

"What?" Rick felt like he was in a speeding car and all four tires had blown at once. "What body bags?"

"I was going to tell you. Allen filled me in. Both bodies in the carriage house were in airtight bags, like they use in disasters or in combat. That's what fouled up the time of death estimate from the coroner. Some doms use them in bondage play. That's what's happening here." He nodded to the movie.

Sandra nodded. "Makes sense. Is that why there wasn't any stench of rotting flesh?"

"It's more complicated than that. It seems...."

Sandra waved her hand as the scene changed again. "Shush, now. Who's that? What's she doing?" A man, naked except for a leather hood encasing his head, lay stretched, spread-eagled, on the bed. A woman, dressed in spiked heels, tight leather shorts, and a bodice, strutted around him, lashing away with a whip that ended in what looked like a horse's tail.

"That's a cat o' nine tails. It's a mild torture device."

"My God, look! That's Victoria!" Rick's universe whirled about him and took on a new, even more macabre orientation. "She told me she had affairs. I never dreamed she was a pervert."

Brandon's fingers dug into his shoulders. "It's not perverted, not really. It's just a different way to have fun with another person."

"You really did this stuff? With that repulsive old pig?"

"Does it matter what I did before we met?" His voice trembled, and his gaze wavered.

Sandra's face was grim. "What matters right now is who's the man on the bed. I'm pretty sure I recognize him."

Rick looked from her to Brandon and then back at the screen. "I can't believe this. Shit! Look where she's tying that shoelace! Doesn't that hurt?"

The scene flickered again, and this time Victoria wore only her leather bodice. The same man lay chained to the bed, but now she straddled his face, her hips rocking back and forth. Rick felt the fascination some people feel watching a car wreck. "What's she doing now? Forcing him to do oral sex? Can't we just turn this off? It's like watching a horrible porno, but with my friggin' dead wife as the star."

"If you can't stand watching, leave. I want to see who the man is. He's not wearing the hood anymore." Sandra peered at the screen and the camera panned closer, revealing his face. "I thought so." She clicked on pause. "Look. It's that bastard Brian. I told you his tastes were disgusting."

"Who?" Rick stared at the screen. "I think you're right. That's Brian Steadman. I guess that must be the connection to Victoria. But this just makes things worse for me! This gives me motive to kill *both* of them." His ability to be surprised seemed to have been used up because he felt nothing at this last revelation.

Brandon's tenor floated into the room like a dove above a riot. "I have a question."

Sandra looked like she could spit at the screen, but she turned to stare at him. "What is it, dear?"

"The camera just panned to a close-up. That means someone else is in that room, photographing this whole thing. Who would that be?"

Sandra's face paled and she stared back at the screen. "You're right. The earlier camera cut could have been Victoria or Brian editing the original video, but someone else had to be there to get that close-up of his face. Who, indeed?"

Chapter Eighteen

"Jail House Rock"

Brandon closed his eyes and inhaled the clean, chlorine scent from the hot tub. His body floated in a languid torpor while the steamy waters roiled about him. His muscles ached from his workout, and his mind longed for sleep. Worry over the events of the last three days churned at his gut, and fatigue dulled his thoughts. He sucked in a deep breath and ducked underneath the surface, letting the jets eddy against his face. It was so quiet there, almost womblike. He yearned for peace.

After what seemed a dark eternity, he burst back to the surface and inhaled a gasp of humid air. Water streamed over his features and burned his eyes. He reached for a towel and swiped his face dry before relaxing again into the liquid whirls.

On the other side of the room, the swimming pool glimmered blue and green under the fluorescent lighting. The pure white ceramic tiles marched across the floor in perfect columns, cascading over the edge and into the deep end, making him think of lemmings. On the other side of the glass wall, Sandra labored with the Nautilus machine in the weight room. He waved and motioned for her to join him. She waved back, pointed at her watch, and held up one finger. He read her lips. "One minute."

He nodded and let his head loll back. Visions of a decomposing body welled up in his mind, an echo of a nightmare from last night. The corpse's flesh sagged in rotting clumps, and maggots fed on exposed muscles. Worse, the smiling face on the grisly vision was the same as in Victoria's portrait upstairs in the hallway outside his room.

Sandra's voice broke his reverie. "Penny for your thoughts."

He gave her a shaky grin. "Just thinking. I've watched too much *CSI*. I can't get the image of those bodies out of my head. I couldn't have been more than thirty feet from them on Christmas Day, and didn't know it."

"Lots of people were in the carriage house in the last nine months, and no one saw them. There was nothing you could do."

"I know. It still creeps me out."

"Try not to think about it. I don't." She shook her head. "I'm going to take a quick shower and change into a swimsuit. Save me a place?"

"Sure." He watched her head to the ladies' room. When the door closed, he dunked his head underwater again before slumping back. Exhaustion dragged at his eyelids.

He jumped at her voice. "Brandon, honey. You shouldn't sleep in the hot tub. You might drown."

"I must have drifted off. I haven't been sleeping well."

"I guess none of us have." The waters sloshed as she settled opposite him. "Oh, that feels so good. I do hate working out."

"You're in real good shape, for...I mean; you're in real good shape."

Her eyes twinkled at him. "I'm going to give you the benefit of the doubt and assume you were going to say 'you're in good shape for a girl.'"

"I was. What else would I say?"

"You're such a dear. I'm just feeling my age, I guess. I thought you were going to say 'old woman.'"

"You're not old at all! You're exactly Rick's age, aren't you?"

She nodded. "In the prime of life, if you're a man. So they tell me. How is Rick doing?"

"I'm worried about him. He's been taking sleeping pills at night, but I don't think he's really resting. He thrashes around in the bed, and he calls out for Victoria."

Concern pooled in her eyes. "Poor Brandon. That must be so hard for you. No wonder you can't sleep, dear." Her foot stroked his shin. "Maybe you should take one of his pills."

"I did. Last night. I won't do *that* again. I had these horrible nightmares. I was back with Peter, and he had me tied up in his dungeon. He told me he had a surprise for me, and then unfolded these body bags, like the ones we saw in that video."

"God, any dream with Peter Warren is a nightmare. I get the heebie-jeebies just thinking of him. Why on earth were you with that old monster, anyway?"

"I thought I was in love with him." He kept his voice diffident. "He was nice to me. He gave me things, took me places. He paid for my tuition at school. I thought he cared for me. But then, when we were in Sedona last summer, I realized I was just...well, *furniture* to him. Something bought and paid for. I moved out as soon as we got back to Chicago."

"You're not furniture to Rick. He really cares for you."

"I thought so. But when we came here, he seemed different, somehow. Distant. Like he was ashamed of me."

"Oh, Brandon, he's ashamed of himself! Think what it must be like for him to be here with you, in Victoria's home and with Victoria's servants. Her presence permeates this place, and he put you in the middle of it. He's guilty about being gay and being married. He's probably even guilty about being guilty, since he loves you." She shook her head. "He's had too many shocks in the last year. Thank God he's got you."

"I do want him to be happy. But I think he misses her, sometimes, too."

"He cared for her, you know, even though she was a horrid witch."

His fingers played with water, trailing a path along the bubbling surface. "I can tell it hurts him when you talk about her that way." He avoided looking at her.

"I know. I shouldn't do it. I guess there's a bit of Victoria in me. We were sisters, after all. Maybe I'm kind of a witch, too." She dimpled. "Will you help me do better?"

He glanced up and shook his head. "You don't need any help. He told me he couldn't have gotten through the last year without you." He swirled his arms in the water, luxuriating in the feel. "I looked on the web for that women's clinic we found in Victoria's appointment book."

Her eyebrows went up. "And?"

"It's an abortion clinic."

"You're kidding. You think she had an abortion?"

"How would I know? I never met the woman. She's your sister."

She seemed about to speak, but the phone shrilled. "Damn that thing. It's got to be Daniels pestering us about something. Would you mind getting it? It's way across the room, and I just got comfortable."

"Sure. I'm turning into a prune anyway." Water gushed off him as he pulled himself out of the tub and picked up a towel. He rushed to the phone, drying himself as he went. "Hello?" He cradled the phone between his head and his shoulder. He glanced at Sandra and, feeling exposed in just his Speedo bikini, wrapped the towel about his waist.

James' voice piped from the other end. "Sir, Mr. Collier asked if you might come to the foyer."

"Rick asked? Sure. I'm in my swimsuit though, so it'll take me a minute to change."

"Sir, I think you're needed right away. Perhaps you could wear a robe?"

"Uh, I think I used the last clean one last night. If it's important, I'll just wrap a towel around my waist."

"I'm sure that will be fine, sir. Is Miss Sandra possibly there with you?"

"Yeah, we were soaking in the hot tub."

"She's needed, too."

"Okay. I'll tell her. We'll be right there." He hung up the phone and frowned.

Sandra's voice echoed against the room's hard surfaces. "What's wrong, Brandon?"

"Rick wants us at the foyer right away, for some reason. James said to not change, just come pronto."

"Well, I will not show up there in my swimming suit." She climbed out of the tub and strode to the women's dressing room. "You tell him he can wait five minutes while I get presentable."

"All right. I'm going to head on up." He hitched the towel tighter, looped another over his shoulders, and headed for the stairs.

He paused in the hallway outside the entryway, and a black hole of panic sucked at his stomach. Sam Sondergard, dressed in his undersheriff's uniform, stood there with two deputies, chatting with Rick, who held some papers in his hands.

"The warrant's in order, as you can see, Mr. Collier."

Rick's hands trembled, but his voice was steady. "It seems to be. I just can't believe it."

"The young man confessed to everything, sir, including his arrangements with Daniels."

Daniels! Relief flooded through Brandon. *Maybe they're not here for Rick!* He stepped forward. "Hi, Sam. What's going on?" He wanted to hold Rick's hand, but he settled for just standing next to him.

Sam's fingers touched the tip of his Smokey the Bear hat. "Hello, Brandon. Sorry to see you under these circumstances. We're here to arrest Daniels for conspiracy to sell a controlled substance and to search his office and quarters."

"You're kidding? Daniels? What controlled substance?" Brandon thought for a second. "Meth?"

Rick's head jerked around to look at him. "How did you know?"

"It just clicked into place when Sam said controlled substance. I mean, he's been acting like a tweaker the whole time I've known him. All of a week, I admit, but I should have seen it."

"How so? I didn't see anything but his usual ass-hat self."

"Well, he was always jittering around, like he couldn't hold still. James told me he flew into a rage over little things, like the broken figurine. And Sandra, or someone, told me his behavior had changed over the last year. More overbearing." Brandon paused. "Oh, and one more thing. He was always scratching at himself. I remember his wrist was raw from it. Tweakers always have bad skin. I would have put it together sooner if we'd been in Chicago. It just didn't occur to me, here in God's country."

Sam grinned at him. "You're a pretty sharp cookie, Brandon, to have put that all together so quickly."

"Well, the shelter I lived in when I was in high school had a floor for meth addicts. They were all just like him." He frowned. "Conspiracy to sell, you said? He was a *dealer?*"

"No. But he let his dealer use the carriage house to meet customers. That's how we learned about all of this. The dealer was the one who set off the fireworks New Year's Eve that set the place ablaze. When we searched his place, looking for illegal fireworks, we found a meth house instead. Right here in Lindermont." Sam shook his head. "I can't believe they were doing this right under my nose."

Brandon looked around and shivered. "So, where's Daniels?"

"I've got some deputies looking through the mansion for him. His car's still in the back. We'll find him."

Sandra walked in and hooked arms with Rick. "I guess this means we can finally fire the SOB?"

Rick stared at her. "I hadn't thought that far ahead. Of course we'll fire him. But he'll be in jail anyway, right, Sam?"

The undersheriff nodded. "If he's found guilty, he'll be sent away for a year or so. For now, though, I bet he's out on bail in no more than two days. The conspiracy charge might not stick, but we've got him on possession. The officer searching his car out back already found his stash and radioed in to me."

Sandra locked eyes with Sam. "Tell me, *Undersheriff,* why it was necessary for you to roust Brandon and me from our hot tub? The poor boy is standing here half naked in this cold hallway."

"I'm sorry about that, ma'am. It was a precaution. Sometimes meth users get violent. They're not predictable. I wanted you all here, where I could protect you."

Brandon nodded. "That seems like a good idea. There was this one guy at the shelter who just went berserk one night, with no warning. He broke a glass in the dining hall and cut a couple of guys up before a bunch of us grabbed him. He fought like a madman."

Sandra nodded. "I see. I'm sorry, Sam. I shouldn't have doubted you."

"It's all right. Perfectly normal question. Nobody likes the cops showing up with warrants." His walkie-talkie buzzed, and he held it to his ear. He nodded, and then spoke. "Good. Bring him to the front, and we'll take him away." He looked at Rick. "They got him. He was hiding in Victoria's rooms, and we found his drug stash. We're done here. You can go on about your business, if you like. Thank you for your cooperation, and we're sorry to have had to disturb you."

"It's all right, Sam. If it had to happen, I'm glad it was you here and not someone else."

"Yes, sir." Sam wrote something on a notepad. "Oh, while I think of it. Do you happen to know if there's any guns on the estate?"

Rick did a double take. "Not so far as I know. When Victoria's father passed away, we donated all his hunting rifles to the local museum."

"Steadman was killed by a gunshot to the head. We don't have any ballistics, so we have no idea what kind, but our best guess, from the size of the entrance wound, is a forty caliber. Nothing like that around here?"

"I hope not. I don't like guns."

Brandon thought about the revolver in the video yesterday, but said nothing.

"We'd like to look around, if you don't mind. Just in case there's one around you forgot about or missed."

Rick nodded his head. "Go ahead and look around, if you want."

Sandra stepped forward. "Just a second, Sam. Do you have a warrant to search for a gun?"

"No. I don't need one, since Rick just gave permission."

"He doesn't have the authority to give permission. As of now, I own Lindermont, and I do not consent to a search. We've had enough disturbances for today."

Sam frowned and looked at Rick. "What's she talking about?"

"I'm not sure."

"Rick, honey, think. You've handled dozens of estates."

He stared at Sandra. "All right. You and Victoria owned Lindermont Manor together, ever since your mother died, right?"

"Right. Same as with the Montgomery Holdings Trust."

He nodded. "I'm Victoria's heir, so when her will goes through probate, I'll inherit her half. But right now, it's her estate that controls her interest. Our wills both name Owen Tellefson, the bank's General Counsel, as executor. So, he acts for her estate. Technically, I can't legally consent since I have no standing. Sam, in order to get permission for a search, you'll have to have both Owen and Sandra agree."

She nodded. "Exactly. I knew you'd see right through this." She glared at the undersheriff and spoke in precise tones. "To be clear, you can't search unless I agree, and I don't consent. You can't go on a fishing expedition and disrupt our home. You've got to have probable cause, and you don't. You should know that, Sam." She scowled. "Is that why you rousted us from the pool to come here? Did you think that we'd be too confused and scared and would just cave in?"

Rick shook his head. "That seems unreasonable, Sandra."

She stomped her foot. "Rick, look at yourself. You haven't slept since this whole mess started. And poor Brandon's the same way. If you won't take care of yourself, someone has to. Starting right now, that someone's going to be me. Your lives are upset enough as it is, without policemen poking around your home and asking you questions." Her eyes snapped at Sam. "When you have probable cause to search Lindermont Manor, come back. Otherwise, please just leave us alone."

Sam nodded. "That's your right, of course." He pursed his lips and put a hand on Rick's shoulder. "May I speak to you as a friend?"

"Certainly."

"We're still at the start of this investigation. It's inevitable that we'll have to look at you as a suspect. You know that, I hope."

"I expected it. That's why I wanted to give permission to search, to clear myself as soon as possible."

"I understand, but Sandra's got a good point. Rick, speaking as your friend, I'd get myself a good criminal attorney. The DA is already all over this case, and he'd like nothing better than a high-profile conviction. You need someone in your corner who understands these things."

"Thanks, Sam. I'll look into it."

Brandon pulled the towel tighter about his shoulders as a chill breeze wafted over him. He watched in silence while four officers clattered down the stairs leading a sullen Daniels to the front door. Their eyes locked for a moment, and a sneer snaked across the estate manager's narrow features before one of the burly deputies jerked him forward. Brandon shook his head. *Poor guy. I wonder what life will be like for him now.*

Chapter Nineteen

"I Still Haven't Found What I'm Looking For"

Rick looked up as Fran MacDonald swept into the waiting room of her law office. Her gray, knee-length winter coat trailed after her like a cape, and her wind-tousled hair bounced with each step.

"Rick, good to see you. Sorry I'm late." She handed her briefcase and wrap to her assistant. "Carl, get me some coffee and a sandwich, would you? I've been in court all day, and I'm famished."

"Sure thing, Fran. Mr. Collier's file is on your desk. The alderman called, and Judge Tabor wants to speak with you." He handed her a sheaf of memos. "Those two numbers are on top; the rest aren't urgent."

She shuffled through the pile. "Be a dear and tell the alderman I'll call him tomorrow." She glanced at Rick in between memos. "I've got to speak to the judge. Just go on into the conference room, and I'll be there in two shakes." She bustled into her private office, and the door slammed after her.

Carl gave Rick a rueful look. "She's like that when she's getting ready for trial. Would you care for anything from the deli downstairs? Their Reubens are great."

"No, thanks, I've eaten. I would have some more coffee, if that's not too much trouble."

"No problem." He opened a door into a spacious conference room. "Just have a seat, and I'll bring it right to you."

Rick reflected that the conference room was both large enough and luxurious enough for a royal audience, which meant that it was modest by modern corporate standards. The Wrigley Building gleamed in the sunlight just a block away, and the John Hancock Center peeked over the skyline. The polished maple conference table sat on a floor inlaid with Italian marble, and a print of Escher's *Ascending and Descending* hung on one wall.

Carl appeared with a carafe of coffee on a serving tray that included sugar, fresh cream, and delicate porcelain cups. "Here you go, sir. You sure you wouldn't care for anything from the deli?"

"I'm good, really." Rick fixed a cup of coffee, settled into a plush, leather conference chair, and waited.

Fran burst into the room carrying a thick folder with color-coded tabs sticking out of it. "Jeez, what a day! How are you doing?" She slapped the folder on the table and ran her fingers through her tangled locks. "God, this wind plays havoc with everything." She fished a couple of pins out of the pocket of her skirt and stuck them in her mouth while her hands tugged her hair into a messy ponytail. The hairpins muffled her words. "How you holding up? Fix me some java, will you? One sugar, no cream."

"Good enough, I guess." Rick moved to serve her.

Her hair adjusted, she flipped through the file. "What a mess. This case has the FBI, the

SEC, and your local cops all over it. Each of 'em are busy whippin' it out to see which one's biggest. That's good for us."

"How so?"

"It'll slow 'em down a bit, and it makes everything more complicated. Actually, that undersheriff of yours is the only professional one in the bunch. He's been forthcoming and gave me an organized file on what he's got. Not like those jerkwads with federal badges."

"Sam's a good man." Rick sighed. "So, what do you know? Are they going to charge me?"

"That jerk-off DA is hot to trot, I can tell. I'd say they'll charge someone in the next week or so. They don't really have a case, and your guy Sam knows it. What we need to do is give them an alternate theory of the crime. That's where I come in. Your sister-in-law was pretty shrewd having you hire me."

"Sandra's quite clever. I recall you did a brilliant job defending the alderman last year."

"Thanks. But that's not why she's smart. I'm already all over Steadman, since I'm defending your buddy Darren at Axinon where he was CEO. I've been through discovery with the feds on that case, and it'll help with this one, since Steadman's one of the DBs. That's cop-speak for dead body. You know, they figure he was killed elsewhere and moved to the carriage house later?"

"No, I didn't. How would they know that?"

"They can't *know* much of anything, with these crimes happening so long ago. What they do know is he was killed by a gunshot that blew out the back of his skull. It's pretty hard to completely clean up a scene where that kind of thing happens, and there was no evidence in the carriage house of blood, bone, or bullets. In addition, there was a fitted rubber sheet, like they use in hospitals and S&M play, stuffed in his body bag. It *did* have bone fragments in it, so they figure the killer stuffed his body and the sheet into a body bag and moved it to the basement of the carriage house. He was pretty small for a guy, so almost anyone in reasonable shape could have done it."

Rick swallowed the saliva that flooded his mouth and hoped he didn't vomit. "God, that's sickening."

"Bastard had it coming, if you ask me. He ripped off pension funds."

"I've read some about that. He was tied up with the Madoff scandal too, right?"

"He was a front for Madoff, among other things. Lots of people wanted a piece of our Mr. Steadman. Problem is, no one knew he was in the good old U.S. of A."

"Sam told me he had a fake ID."

"Yeah." She turned to a tab in the file. "He entered the U.S. from Geneva last March first, travelling under a Slovenian passport issued to one Josip Krizman. He had a Swiss driver's license in that name, and credit cards, too, from...." She peered at the file. "The Schweizer Privatbank für Investitions und Sparungs, in Zurich. Ever hear of it?"

"Not that I recall. We do business with a number of Swiss banks. If it's a private investment bank, it would have had a pretty exclusive clientele."

"Steadman seems to have had a couple hundred million stashed away with them. Funny thing about the Swiss privacy laws on banking. They make this big exception if there's evidence of fraud against a bank. They don't take kindly to folks who rip off financiers."

"So I hear. What was Steadman, or Krizman, or whatever, doing back in the U. S.?"

"No one knows." She closed the file. "It looks like he was having an affair with your wife. Did you know that?"

"Not at the time. But after she disappeared, lots of nasty rumors came back to me. That was one of them."

"Well, that one seems to be true. There're security tapes of them checking into the Drake here in town for overnight trysts, for example. And then there's the playroom in the basement of The Spike, over on Clark Street."

Rick frowned. "What?"

"You ever hear of it?" She shoved a photo across the table.

"It looks like some sleazy porn store." He lifted his eyes. "Whatever could that have to do with Victoria?"

"She and her buddy Steadman were regular customers, buying S&M gear." She grinned at him. "My PI's good. He's gonna cost you plenty. Anyway, there're more security videos showing both of them in the store. Steadman even stopped there on March first, when he got to Chicago, and bought some crap. The basement's all tricked out as a dungeon that people can rent, and they were regulars there too."

Rick thought of the movie they'd seen. "Honest. I swear I had no idea Victoria was into that kind of thing. Is that the place we saw on that movie?"

"Nah, doesn't match the video at all. They must have had some other place fixed up, maybe out of town. My PI's looking for it. That was another smart move by Sandra, having you give that SD card to me instead of the cops."

"I don't get it. Won't you have to give it to them?"

"It's privileged. If they subpoena it, we'd probably have to give it up. I suppose they'll find out eventually, since Sandra and that kid, what's his name?"

"Brandon."

"Yeah, him. Eventually the cops'll ask the right question and it'll come out that we've got it. I might surrender it sooner, since there's nothing really incriminating on it."

"I don't want Brandon involved."

"Honey, he's living at your house and he's seen that movie. He's involved. They're gonna talk to him. I've already got his statement, and I've been clear he's to tell the cops the absolute truth about everything. I won't suborn perjury. That's why you can't testify, if it comes to trial. I don't want you talking to the police at all without me present."

"Why? I don't have anything to hide. Won't hiding just make me look worse?"

She shook her head. "For a millionaire banker, you sure can be naïve. Whatever happens, we don't want the cops to know you found her body. They know the two of you fought, but apparently no one saw you go to the carriage house that day. At least, it's not in anyone's statements, and I've been over them like white on rice."

"I didn't say anything back then because I was sure I'd be charged with her murder."

"Good thinking. Sandra and that kid, Brandon, might have to tell the cops what you told them, but it's hearsay, and you're not talking." She turned to another tab. "How about this abortion clinic. You know anything about that?"

"God, no! Victoria was opposed to abortion and gave money to right-to-life groups. When I found out, I gave equal amounts to Planned Parenthood."

"Well, she had two appointments, about a week apart last February, at this clinic. All they do there is abortions. The rest of their practice is elsewhere, to protect their other patients from the picketers. We can't get her records, but it's pretty clear she must have had one. You think Steadman might be the father?"

"I don't see how. She told me she was going to Switzerland to have her lover's baby. Didn't you say Steadman had a Swiss driver's license and bank account?"

"Yeah. So, if it wasn't his baby, then whose was it?" She made a note in the file. "If we find out, it could provide motive. See, we've got to come up with a credible theory of the crime that includes someone else as the murderer."

Rick sighed and couldn't meet her eyes. "I suppose it doesn't look good."

"I've seen worse. There're a lot of unknowns here, and since they can't nail down the time of death that'll make any case tough to prosecute."

Carl knocked and entered. "Here's your sandwich, Fran. Corned beef on rye. I got onion rings and a cherry Coke, too." He turned to Rick. "Can I get you anything, sir? More coffee?"

"I'm good, thanks."

"That'll be all, Carl. I'll ring if we need something." She took a huge bite and wiped her mouth. "You mind if I slip off my shoes? My feet are killing me." She turned to another tab in her file with one hand while rubbing her left sole with the other. "The timeline on this is all screwed up. Want an onion ring?"

Rick shook his head.

"These things are marvelous. Probably turn my blood to orange sludge, but it'll be worth it. Given what you saw in the carriage house, our working assumption has to be that Victoria died the night of March thirteenth. The last person to see her alive was Maury Saliba, the contractor working on the carriage house. He says she screamed at him for about five minutes, and he walked out. After that, nada."

"So someone went to the carriage house and killed her. They left, I went there and found the body, and then they came back and, and...."

"And stuffed her and a couple of gallons of insecticide in a body bag and buried the whole thing under a pile of coal. Except that her death might have been an accident. COD was a cervical fracture at C3, most consistent with a fall. Of course, she might have been pushed, too. Given that the body was hidden, the cops are going with pushed."

"But why leave and come back?"

"I figure the murderer left to get the body bag. The place was full of pesticide, which may have given him the idea for hiding the corpse, especially if they'd seen the cop show that used this same method."

Rick shuddered. "That's gruesome."

"Yup. Cold blooded, too. But the interesting question has to do with when Steadman was killed. One possibility is that it was later. Maybe days later."

"How do you figure?"

"Look, someone had to move the money the next morning, right?"

Rick nodded.

"We know for sure it wasn't you, and the cops know it too." She glanced at file while chewing on her sandwich. "This guy James Sanger gave them a statement that he checked in on you every couple of hours that night. Seems you'd been drinking and taking sleeping pills, and he was worried about you."

"Yeah. I told you about that."

"Uh-huh. You must have been depressed over your fight with your wife. At least that's what the cops seem to think. Anyway, it means someone else moved the money the next morning. At the time, you all thought Victoria did it, since only her fingerprints were on her computer. But now you and I know she was dead back in the carriage house, and thus she couldn't have done it. So who did?"

"How should I know?"

She leafed through her folder again. "Doesn't that damned bank of yours have security cameras? Weren't there tapes of who went in and out of the executive offices that morning?"

"There should have been. Someone bollixed up the system. The tapes were all missing."

"How convenient. Who could have done that?"

"The guards, of course. But the control console was in a closet off the foyer. We all knew it was there, so any number of people could have taken the tapes, including Victoria."

"Uh-huh. How about Daniels?"

Rick snorted. "Daniels? So far as I know, he's never even been to Chicago, let alone to the bank. He certainly wouldn't have known any codes or anything about the security system."

"Uh-huh." She made another note in her file. "Well, if Victoria was in cahoots with someone, he would have known too. Whoever moved the money probably also fouled up the tapes. Interesting." Her fingers made a rat-a-tat-tat sound on the table. "Back then, you all must have thought Victoria hid the tapes. Why would she do that? It was basically her money, right?"

"Sandra knew she'd been having an affair. We figured her lover was with her that morning, and they didn't want to leave a trail back to him. There were two half-empty coffee cups in her office. If the cups had been there the day before, the janitors would have cleaned them up."

"I guess that made sense then. But now we know it couldn't have been Victoria, since she was dead in the carriage house. If there were two people there, who were they?" She tapped the arm of her chair with her pen. "Maybe there was just one person, and he wanted us to think there were two. But that doesn't make sense either." She made a note. "Anyway, one possibility is that Steadman moved the funds."

"Steadman? We thought he might be there, but not that he'd moved the money. Why do you think it might be him?"

"Lots of reasons. First, you remember his rental car? Someone dropped it off that morning at one of the rental company's offices on La Salle. Second, the money went to the Banque Internationale de Crédit in the Caymans. That's one of the banks that Steadman used to move his Axinon money offshore. Third, we know he and Victoria were lovers, so he may have known her account numbers and passcodes. Fourth, there were no fingerprints."

Rick tried to keep the exasperation out of his voice. "How can no fingerprints be evidence?"

"Latex gloves hide fingerprints." She held up a copy of a charge slip. "Steadman bought both latex gloves and body bags at that S&M store on Clarke Street when he got to Chicago on March first. If he hadn't turned up dead, he'd be the ideal suspect."

"Maybe he killed her and then stole the money? You said it went to a bank he'd used before."

"Not likely he'd take the risk, not when he's already got hundreds of times that much squirreled away from his swindle at Axinon. In fact, if she was gonna run off with him, it's hard to see why she'd move the money, either." She finished her sandwich and munched on an onion ring. "What we gotta do is find another suspect, one with means, motive, and opportunity. So, let's get back to the timeline. All his money goes out of your bank at seven in the morning, and no one notices until noon?"

"We would have noticed when we closed out for the day. It was a large amount, but lots of money goes in and out of our bank. It was pure chance we caught it before close of business."

"So talk to me."

"Well, Sandra had been at Montgomery College the day before and made a pledge for remodeling a student lounge. The next day, the day the money got moved, she dropped by the bank and asked one of the trust officers to move some funds to the College's Foundation. That's when he noticed most of the cash was gone from her trust."

She looked at her file again, and her eyebrows went up. "That's a hell of a lot of money to have in cash. I'd have thought that most of the Trust would be held in investments."

"It wasn't cash, it was a demand deposit, like a savings account. We'd been moving money around for several months. Even back then, it was obvious that the market was going to crater, so we were repositioning our investments. The transfer just happened to coincide with a time when we had a lot of liquidity."

"So someone moves this fortune in cash off to the Caymans. Then what?"

"Then nothing. The bank in the Caymans told us they'd gotten another order about five minutes later to transfer it to another bank. They said their banking privacy laws forbade them to reveal where. They wouldn't even reveal the name of their account holder, the one that got the money. Sam did some checking with the police down there, someone he went to school with, and we think it was Victoria, but we weren't sure."

She nodded. "Typical money laundering. At this point, who knows where it went?" She scowled. "The SEC has done some checking, and it turns out this bank no longer exists."

"You're kidding."

"Supposedly, Hurricane Gustav destroyed the bank *and* its backup data center last August. The feds think that someone involved in Steadman's swindle might have bribed the bank's officers to lose the records, since he also used it to move Axinon money. In any case, the records are gone. It's anyone's guess where the Montgomery money wound up that morning."

"Can't the CIA or someone find out? This is outrageous! That was nearly a third of the Trust."

"I'm sure the CIA knows. There's a record kept by the Society for Worldwide Interbank Financial Telecommunication in Belgium. Two years ago, the FBI or the SEC could have issued a National Security Letter and gotten that information, but that's all tightened up now. There's no evidence of terrorism, so no NSL. The information is lost." She wadded up the remains of her meal. "Problem is, if Steadman moved the money, why did he do it, and how does he wind up dead in your carriage house? If I were the DA, I'd figure you killed him since he was boinking your wife and stole from your bank."

"But I didn't!"

"I know, I know. So maybe someone else moved the money." She pursed her lips. "You know, it might have been part of the cover-up of the murders. Maybe the killer didn't want or need the money, and just moved it to make it look like Victoria had run off. If that's right, it worked. You all figured she'd done it."

"I guess."

"Yeah, well in any case, your buddy the undersheriff was still suspicious last spring. But he didn't have any evidence of real foul play, since she had authority to move the money. You and Sandra were the aggrieved parties, so he had to drop it." She shook her head. "Let's start with a working hypothesis that someone else moved the money. It's too much of a coincidence for Steadman's rental car to show up that same day a couple of blocks from your bank, so that means he must have been killed the same night as Victoria. Maybe the killer used his rental car to move his body to the carriage house and then drove in to Chicago and did the transfer as a cover-up."

"I guess. But who would have done it?"

"For sure, lots of people wanted a piece of Steadman, except no one knew he was here. Not to speak ill of the dead, but your wife wasn't the most beloved person on the planet, either. Maybe it was one of her jilted lovers. Maybe it was the father of her aborted fetus." Her fingers drummed on the table. "If the killer murdered Victoria and left the carriage house to get the body bags, then maybe he knew about the dungeon in that movie." Her palm slapped onto the table. "It has to be third person in the room when that video was made, the one running the camera! There was a *ménage a trios*, and they had a falling-out. That'll be our alternate theory of the crime."

"It sounds kind of slim to me."

"All we have to do is provide reasonable doubt. This case is so fucked up, there's reasonable doubt all over the place. If we play our cards right, the jury will hate the two victims and be looking for reasons to find you innocent."

"Unless it comes out that I'm gay."

"Yeah, there's that. We'll have to take our chances on that."

"Won't we have to know who that third person is? The one running the camera?"

"No, all we have to do is provide a credible argument that someone other than you is the killer, an alternative theory of the crime that's believable. The one running that camera is our man."

"So why won't they just argue it was me running the camera?"

She flipped through the file again. "That video had a date on it, the previous November sometime. It was displayed in the video itself and embedded inside the MPEG file. Where were you at that time?"

"I spent part of October and all of November in Dallas, handling an acquisition for the bank."

"So you'll have lots of witnesses. Good. This might work out to our advantage after all."

Rick scowled. "I don't understand why I'm the only suspect. Why aren't the cops looking at Daniels?"

She lifted somber eyes in his direction. "Maybe they are."

"Look, he was having an affair with her. That's what started our fight that day. I fucking caught him getting dressed in her rooms, and she was naked in her bed. He scuttled out, and we fought. Where the hell was *he* the rest of that day?"

"According to him, he went to his rooms and mainlined on meth. He says he was out of it until the next day. No one else saw him the day of the murder, but both that Sanger fellow and the cook, Emma Joyner, saw him about eight the next morning."

"So he doesn't have an alibi for the night of the murders. Aren't meth users violent?"

She nodded. "Sometimes."

"Well, then. There's your alternate theory of the crime. He's the one running the camera. When he found out she was going to run off with Steadman, he flew into a drug-induced rage and killed the both of them."

"That's certainly possible. It seems to fit the majority of the facts." She closed her file. "If he was running the camera, he would know about the dungeon and the body bags. We've got to find that damned sex dungeon. I've got this gut feeling that's the key to this case."

Chapter Twenty

"Smoke Gets in Your Eyes"

Brandon huddled at Victoria's desk and read the last sentence in his zoology text for the third time. He sighed and glanced at his cell phone resting beside his open book. The keypad beckoned and his fingers reached out to touch the star and the two as he thought of Rick. Uncertainty gripped him, and Allen's invitation to call anytime echoed in his mind. Hesitant fingers picked up his phone and punched star followed by three instead.

He jumped when James knocked at the open door. "Hi, there. What's up?" He slid his phone into his shirt pocket, the call to Allen incomplete.

"Sir, Emma fixed a sandwich and a glass of milk for you. We were worried that you weren't eating." He placed the silver serving tray on the desk and unfolded a crisp linen napkin.

"Thank you, James. Please tell Emma thanks, too." He took a reluctant bite of the sandwich to show his gratitude. "What's that under your arm?"

"Just a trinket, sir. It's the replacement statuette for the one that got broken." He nodded toward the bookcase where Brandon had stored Victoria's other figurines. "Shall I place it over there, sir?"

"Sure, whatever." He took another bite of the sandwich. The taste of food made his jaws ache for more as a sudden hunger gnawed at his body. "This sandwich really does hit the spot."

"Yes, sir." James fidgeted. "Emma and I plan to play a spot of cribbage later. Perhaps, with Mr. Collier gone to Chicago for the night, you'd care to join us?"

"That's really nice of the two of you, James. But you know, I kind of need to study. School starts next week, and I've still got to do my pre-class homework."

"We understand, sir. A lot has happened in the last week. If you change your mind, we'll be in the kitchen." He gave a small bow and departed.

Brandon sighed and sipped at the milk. When his cell phone shrilled, he slopped some onto his textbook in his haste to answer. "Hello?"

Rick's baritone resonated loud and clear in his ear. "Brandon, it's so good to hear your voice."

"How are you? How did the meeting with your attorney go?"

"Not bad. She's studied the evidence, and we're working on what she calls theories of the crime. It's a complicated process."

"I get it. Like Sherlock Holmes. It's inductive reasoning. We do the same thing in science labs. Finding a theory that fits all the facts."

"In this case, the goal is to find a theory that includes someone besides me as the murderer."

Brandon hesitated as the haunting image of Rick killing Victoria lacerated his mind. Desperate to replace that horror with any alternative, he muttered, "Well, I think Daniels is the obvious choice. He's a druggie, and he was having an affair with her."

"Yeah, that's what I think too. Somehow she didn't seem quite convinced."

Brandon's breath caught in his throat, and he almost admitted he wasn't convinced either. "Why not?"

"She didn't exactly say it wasn't him. She just didn't seem certain."

Brandon sighed, wishing for more. "Speaking of Daniels, Sam left a message that he's out on bail."

"Well, that's no surprise." Rick's voice seemed weary. "Fran said to expect it. Oh, by the way, she's hired a private investigator. He might be talking to you."

"Send him on. I had a good feeling about your lawyer after she interviewed me."

"She does inspire confidence. She seems to think that the key to the case is the sex playroom we saw in that movie. Maybe there's more evidence there."

He frowned. "Any clues where it's located?"

"None so far. The PI is looking for it, though." Rick paused. "What are you doing tonight?"

"Homework. James asked me to play cribbage with him and Emma, but I didn't feel like it."

Rick chuckled. "You should go ahead, but don't bet any money. James is a real card shark when it comes to that game." He yawned. "I took a pill when I got to the condo. Maybe I'll get some sleep tonight."

"I sure miss you. This is our first night apart in two months, since I first had dinner with you."

Another yawn gusted from the phone. "I miss you, too. Your picture is right here on my nightstand."

"Sounds like your pill might be kicking in."

"I think so." Fatigue dragged at his voice.

"Well, then, I'll let you go. Call me in the morning?"

"Sure. I love you."

"Love you, too. Night."

When the phone went dead, Brandon slipped it back in his pocket and gazed through the window. The early evening sky faded from crimson in the west to deep purple overhead. A few stars glittered in the heavens, and wisps of clouds on the horizon threatened a winter storm. The nagging fear that Rick was a killer hung over him. His heart longed to believe it was someone else, anyone else. But his mind, ever analytic, kept sifting the evidence and, like Banquo's ghost, whispered Rick's name in his ear. Brandon knew he had means and opportunity. Jealousy and fear of exposure each were compelling motives. No matter how he thought about it, no one else had as much of an incentive to murder.

His eyes roamed the room and fell on the statue of Eros, now shimmering in a beam of dwindling sunlight. A brief smile pulled his lips up as he recalled their time together last night. But the memory of his hurt at Rick's reaction when he'd admitted concealing the broken figurine darkened his mood once again.

In retrospect, it seemed so silly to have hidden the shattered statue. He remembered his panic, sweeping the pieces in the drawer and hiding them. As those images cascaded through his vision, in a flash he recalled the key hanging in the well of the desk. Certain that it was important, he clawed the drawer open and, on his knees, peered into the darkness. Yes, it was still there! He pulled it out and placed it on the desk with a clink.

The key fob read "Lindermont Arms, Unit F6, 412 Cycle Club Lane, Dubuque, Iowa." He reached into his pocket and pulled out his keychain. Less than two weeks ago, Daniels had given him the keys to the estate's condo in Dubuque, the one the family used when flying in and out of the airport. That, too, was for Lindermont Arms, but for unit A1. He whipped out his cell phone, opened the GPS navigator, and keyed in the address. Sure enough, it was south of town on Highway Sixty-One, just east of the airport.

He frowned and tapped his forefinger on the polished desktop. Why was this key hidden?

Why were there two condos? Maybe, just maybe, this was where Victoria kept her S&M playroom! He snatched at his phone and called Rick. Rather than hearing his reassuring baritone, it went to voicemail. "Shit." He scrolled through his call history until he found Fran MacDonald's law office. Voicemail again. "Shit, shit, shit." He stared out the window at the gathering darkness while his fingers drummed on the desk. This could be

important, too important to let wait. Maybe
something there would change the weight of
the evidence and let him believe that his lover
wasn't a murderer. He knew what he had to
do. He strode from the room and headed
toward the garage. On the way, he left a quick
voice message with Rick to tell him what he'd
discovered and where he was going.

The tinny voice of the GPS on Brandon's
phone announced, "Turn left on Cycle Club
Lane and drive two hundred feet to your
destination." After making the turn, he pulled
to the side of the street and gazed out the
windshield. The light on the airport tower
flashed on the other side of the highway, and
the city of Dubuque glowed behind the hills to
the north. Empty fields surrounded the little
industrial park, filled with dead corn shocks
that marched in wavy furrows following the
curves of the hillsides. Everything seemed to
shine with an ethereal glow from the full moon
hanging on the horizon.

Dark warehouses huddled on his left,
while on the right a row of *faux* brownstones
clustered behind an empty parking lot. A
battered sign announced he'd arrived at
Lindermont Arms. Parsimonious streetlights
cast a dirty, yellow illumination over the
buildings, and grimy snow piled at the edges
of the walkways. An ornate letter A marked
the front building.

Brandon put his car in gear and edged
forward. Six more buildings lined up behind
building A. Cars stood in the driveways, and
lights glimmered in the second-floor windows
of most of the units in buildings A through D.
Building E seemed to be less than half-

occupied and building F stood dark, with snow drifted over the walks. He pulled into the driveway for unit F6 and put his car in park. The outside temperature monitor on his dashboard glowed with the number twelve, and his car shuddered in a gust of wind rushing across the empty prairie behind the building. He killed his engine, turned up his collar, and entered the frigid night.

The sound of the doorbell chime penetrated to the outside and sang a brief counterpoint to the wail of the winds. He shivered and pounded on the door. When there was no answer, he looked about and used his key. A welcome burst of warm air from the dark interior washed across his face as he hurried inside.

In the sudden darkness, his fingers fumbled for the light switch. A solitary table lamp came on, revealing a nondescript living room that could have been in any of a thousand cheap motels. A small kitchen alcove stood in one corner, and a hall next to the stairs led to the back. He slipped off his coat and draped it on the sofa. This had to be the place. He walked down the hallway, looking for a bedroom. The first door opened into a bath. The second was the prize that he sought.

The red bulbs in the overhead track lights gave everything a threatening, ruddy color. Garbage bags, secured with duct tape, covered the solitary window in the room. A brass double bed, covered with black plastic sheets, dominated the room. Chains dangled from the bedposts, and padded shackles and cuffs rested on the sheets, waiting for the next victim. Other familiar instruments glimmered on the walls. His gaze flitted across the whips, clamps, collars, and related items before it settled on an automatic pistol, sitting on the dresser on his right. The barrel pointed at a framed photograph of a woman wearing the gear of a dominatrix—spiked heels, leather shorts and bra, and a leather officer's cap with a death's head insignia in the front.

Brandon recognized Victoria's features trapped inside the picture frame and shuddered.

An enormous entertainment center, with a plasma TV and assorted A/V equipment, covered one wall. A tripod held a camera that pointed at the bed, waiting to record whatever games might play out. DVDs, with dates scribbled on their white surfaces, lay scattered on the floor nearby. He knelt and shuffled through them with trembling fingers. Then thoughts of fingerprints bubbled in his mind and he dropped them. It didn't matter. This was the place, all right. He reached for his cell phone to try Fran's number again when he spotted the date 03/12/08 on one of the DVDs. That was the day before the murders! He slipped it into the player and started the TV.

The plasma flickered, and then blurry, out-of-focus images flashed across the screen before settling into a shot of the equipment hanging on the wall. The video panned to the foot of the bed, where manacles clamped a man's hairy legs. The person running the camera had a sense of drama, for the image crept upward, exposing his naked body bit by bit and finally ending in a close-up of his face. Brandon gasped to see Daniels bound and gagged on the TV screen.

The speakers rustled and music filled the room, a golden oldie. A woman's voice, speaking with Sandra's intonations but deeper and somehow threatening, came next. "Smoke gets in your eyes. Perfect, Brian. Just what we need for this dog."

On the bed, Daniels whimpered and terror gleamed in his eyes.

Brandon stared in horror as a second naked man knelt on the bed. This one was short and wiry, covered with a mat of curly, dark hair. He reached out and twisted at Daniels' nipples. A muffled scream covered the Platters' mellifluous tones for an instant, and then the woman spoke again.

"That's good, Brian. We need to show him what happens when a dog defies his mistress."

Brian turned to face her. "Tell me what to do, Victoria."

The image jiggled before it steadied into a wide shot of the two men in the bed. Victoria, in her dominatrix gear, sidled into view and ran a lash over Daniels' heaving torso. "I want you to make him into a woman, Brian. Fuck him for me."

Daniels thrashed his body back and forth, but the chains and manacles held him in place. Sweat gleamed on his body, and his eyes were wild with horror.

Victoria pulled a syringe from a table next to the bed and tapped the cylinder. "Just a little moon juice for you, dog, to help you enjoy it." She wound a rubber band around his arm, thumped at his vein, and injected him. Standing back with a feral grin on her face, she turned to her companion. "Now, Brian, do it now! I want to see this little fucker humiliated.

We'll save the DVD and send it to his church cronies if he gives us any trouble."

Tears streamed from Daniels' eyes and his body shook, perhaps from the drugs, perhaps from fear, perhaps from both.

Brandon watched in horror as Brian raped Daniels. The harmonies from the Platters' 1950s hit droned in the background in a macabre counterpoint to the violence on the bed. Sickened and unwilling to watch more, Brandon stopped the DVD. "Fuck me. I guess that gives Daniels motive," he said breathily. Exultation mixed with his revulsion. "That means Rick's not the murderer after all." He reached for the eject button, and jumped at a shout from behind.

"You little fucking faggot! What are you doing here?"

Brandon's moment of triumph exploded. Panic erupted in his gut, and adrenaline rushed from his core out his limbs like electricity through an overloaded circuit. He whirled about to see Daniels standing in the room, his eyes bulging and his face crimson.

"I...I found this key, and I was curious. What they did to you...that was awful." His head whirled, and his thoughts spun out of control. *What to do?*

Daniels raced across the room and snatched up the gun. With a quick slide of the barrel, he chambered a round and pointed it at Brandon. "You saw that video, didn't you? You lousy little fucking *faggot*." Spittle sprayed across the room, and he swiped at his mouth with the back of his hand. His pupils were pinpoints, and the muscles of his face jerked at random intervals.

God, he's totally tweaked out. Careful, boy. "I didn't see anything, honest, just this room. What is this place?"

Daniels' eyes narrowed, and his gaze took on a cunning cant. "If you didn't see anything, then what was so awful? You said what they did to me was awful, so what the fuck did you see?"

"Nothing, honest."

"Stand back." Daniels waved the gun at him and rushed forward. He pushed play on the DVD, and the scene with him bound to the bed started to replay. "You little *fucker!* I came here to destroy that fucking DVD, and now you've seen it!"

"I won't tell anyone, honest. God, they fucking *raped* you. That's awful."

"Shut up! Just shut up. *You're* the fucking faggot here, not me!" A spasm gripped his body and he jerked the gun up to point between Brandon's eyes. "Strip!"

"What?" A black hole of fear coiled in his gut and sucked the breath from his lungs.

"You heard me, faggot. Strip. I'll show you who's a man!"

Brandon held up his hands. "You don't have to do this...."

Daniels flipped the gun to one side and a shot snapped out, thunking into the wall. Acrid smoke drifted from the barrel. "Do it now." He kept his eyes glued to Brandon while he reached for the handcuffs on the bed.

Brandon backed up to the dresser, his hands fumbling with his shirt buttons. The dead weight of his cell phone thumped against his chest. He pulled it out and placed it on the dresser, his eyes on Daniels.

"Come on! Hurry up!" His eyes roamed the room, and he grabbed a whip from the wall.

Brandon took the opportunity to press *3 on his phone and hoped. He pulled off his shirt and used it to hide the glowing screen. Allen answered, and Brandon spoke to cover the sounds from the little speaker. "I don't get it. Why are there two apartments here at the Lindermont Arms? I can understand one, next to the Dubuque airport, but why two?" He prayed his words were enough.

"God, you're a moron, even for a faggot. What do you think it's for? Come on! Strip down." The gun made little circles in the air, always pointed at Brandon.

"What are you going to do with me?"

"I'm going to fuck you, and then I'm going to kill you, queer boy. No one is ever gonna know what they did to me."

"They deserved to die for raping you."

"Shut the fuck up!" He jittered about the room, and the cuffs clanked in his hands. "They're going to burn in hell forever! And they fucking *deserve* it. That bitch! She killed my baby! Did you know that?"

Brandon's eyes widened. "We figured out she must have had an abortion. You were the father?"

"I had to be. That fucking bastard Steadman was out of the country. But then he came back, and she said it was over between us. We had it out, right here in this room, and she told me she'd killed my baby. They both laughed at me, then pulled a gun—*this* gun— and tied me up. Then...then...the fucking bastards!"

"No one will blame you for what happened, after what they did."

"Shut up! No one's going to blame me for anything, because no one's going to know what they did to me. I told you to strip! Do it now!"

Brandon swallowed and slipped off his loafers. He took his time, flexing his muscles. Daniels' eyes never left him, and a trickle of sweat ran down one temple. Hopping on one foot, he removed his socks.

"Come on, come on. Don't take all day!" The gun never wavered, even though the hand holding it was white with tension and shook with fury.

When his pants fell to the floor, he gripped his body with his arms and trembled. Cold sweat congealed on his torso, and fear overwhelmed reason.

Daniels sneered at him. "God, look at your underwear. A fucking bikini, like a woman. Come on, out of those too!"

"Why are you doing this to me? I haven't done anything to you."

"You're a fucking faggot. That's enough of a reason." Another shot snapped out, and the mirror over the dresser shattered. "Come on, finish!"

Brandon let his shorts drop to the floor and kicked them to one side. He covered himself as best he could and waited.

"Get it hard. Jack off."

"What? I don't think I can."

"Do it, fucker, or I'll blow your brains out right now."

Brandon gulped and closed his eyes. His hands felt cold against his genitals, and his heart thudded in his chest. He thought of Rick, of their time together. Fear swallowed desire, and panic killed lust.

After what seemed an endless time, Daniels sneered at him. "What's wrong, queer boy? Can't get it up?"

"I'm sorry...I can't...I'm trying."

"You're fucking worthless, faggot. Hands behind your head. Now! Do it!" His pants tented with his erection, and a wet spot formed on his jeans.

The DVD replayed its saga of violence on the plasma screen. The Platters again started "Smoke Gets in Your Eyes." Brandon obeyed.

"Turn around. Face the wall."

When he turned, his eyes caught the dim glow of his cell phone underneath his shirt. A faint, forlorn spark of hope flickered deep within his soul. *Maybe, just maybe...* Daniels jerked his arms down. The cuffs were cold and bit into his flesh.

"Turn around and look at me."

Brandon faced him and held his head high. "What do you want me to do?"

"God, I hate fucking faggots." He pointed with the gun. "Lay on the bed."

Brandon inched forward, his eyes never leaving the gun. When Daniels started to undo his belt, his aim wavered and Brandon took a chance. He rushed forward and kicked at Daniels' legs. The two tangled for an instant and tumbled to the floor, but not before the gun flared again. The pistol clattered across the room, out of reach. Searing pain ripped through Brandon's left shoulder, and he screamed as he thrashed on the dirty carpet. His ears rang, and the room spun out of control. With a terrifying suddenness, weakness flooded his muscles, and dark blood pooled underneath him.

Daniels' shriek filled the room and drowned out the music from the DVD. "You fucker. You broke my kneecap!" He scuttled across the floor to retrieve his gun. Something thumped and banged, as if from a great distance, and voices shouted out, but Brandon couldn't make out their words.

Daniels lifted himself to his feet and staggered against the entertainment center. The image of Steadman raping him flickered on the television behind him while Jerome Kern's lyrics lilted out of the speakers. Brandon stared into the depths of the barrel of the gun and faced death.

A shot roared, and a neat hole formed in Daniels' forehead. A sound like wet spaghetti hitting a wall followed as his blood and brains splattered all over the flat plasma screen. A uniformed policeman ran into the room, his weapon smoking, and knelt at Brandon's side. "Hang on, kid, help's on the way. He can't hurt you now." His voice came as if from miles away, over the ringing in his ears and the melody from the speakers.

"How?" Brandon's voice croaked from his throat, and his arm was a dead weight underneath the lava flow of pain than engulfed his shoulder.

"It was your cell phone, kid. Your sheriff friend got the call. He phoned Dubuque PD with the location, and we used the GPS in your phone to nail down which apartment. My beat's the airport, so it didn't take me any time at all to get here. Good thing, too, or you'd have been a goner for sure. They piped your phone right to me, so I knew what to expect. That cell phone probably saved your life." His voice was flat, as if he squeezed all the emotion out of it.

A siren wailed in the background, and Brandon's vision faded. His vision dimmed, but his ears still caught the melancholy tones of "Smoke Gets in Your Eyes."

Chapter Twenty-One

"Let It Be"
May, 2009

Brandon strolled along the cobbled Zwingliplatz and inhaled the crisp mountain air. He squeezed Rick's hand, and an impetuous grin tugged at his features. "Zurich is a beautiful city. Thanks for bringing me along."

"I'm glad you could come. Having you here turns a tedious business trip into a vacation. How's your shoulder holding up?"

He lifted the sling that bound his left arm, and a tiny pain pinged deep inside the joint. "I'm doing great. The doctor said that I'll be fully recovered by this time next year."

Rick frowned. "I'm sorry that you had to miss school this spring."

Brandon shrugged and winced at another twinge. "It'll still be there in the fall. Allen promised me I could start work in his lab anytime. I'm just glad that all that is behind us."

"Thanks to you. I really thought they were going to charge me with the murders."

"You mean thanks to Sam. He recorded everything that came through on my cell phone and played it for the DA. That, and the videos, gave him all the headlines he wanted."

"Yeah, then everything came out, the whole messy scandal. The murders, Victoria's affairs, me being gay, everything. The gossips had a field day." He stopped and stared at his lover. "It seems so strange now. Back then, I'd panic at the idea of being out, even after I met you." He let a knuckle skim over Brandon's cheek. "Now it seems like the most natural thing in the world."

Brandon swallowed the lump in his throat and pulled him closer. "I love you, you big lug."

"I love you, too." He leaned forward, and their lips brushed together.

A passerby jostled them, grinned, and muttered, *"Gehen Sie zu es, Geliebtjunge."*

Brandon nodded and smiled. *"Guten tag."* He whispered in Rick's ear, "What did he say?"

His eyes crinkled in response, and a chuckle passed his lips. "Something like, 'Go to it, loverboy.'"

Brandon squeezed his hand. "I guess we were making a spectacle of ourselves."

"Who cares?" He tugged at Brandon's good arm. "We should hurry, or we'll be late."

"Sandra won't mind. She stuck with you through all of this, too. I'm glad she came along with us. We're lucky to have her in our lives."

"I've been lucky on all of this. Without Sam's recording and Daniels' confession, I might be in jail. But your quick thinking saved everything." He shuddered. "I think I'll keep you handcuffed to me, just to be sure you don't ever do anything like that again. I thought the world was going to end when I heard you'd been shot."

Brandon shivered. "Tell you what, I'll just hold on to your hand and we'll skip the handcuffs, okay?"

Rick blushed. "Sorry. I didn't mean to bring those memories back. I just meant that I want us to be together forever."

"Me, too." Brandon decided to change the subject. "Hey, can we stop and get some postcards? The view from the steeple of the Grossmunster was fantastic."

"Sure. We're lucky it's such a clear day. You can't always see the Glarner Alps from old town." He glanced at his watch. "We're supposed to meet Sandra in about thirty minutes. Should I call a cab while you get your cards?"

"I can walk. My legs are fine; it's just my arm that's still bunged up." He flipped through the selection offered by the street vendor. "Sure you can't join us for lunch?"

"I wish. I've got to meet with the president of our correspondent bank at noon. It'll be a boring two hours of wienerschnitzel, beer, and bean counting."

Brandon grinned. "The beer part sounds good."

"Yeah, but you can have that with Sandra and skip the boring numbers." He checked his watch again. "If we're going to walk, we really should be going."

Sandra was waiting outside der Weisser Wind Restaurant. The dual greyhound logo of the banker's guild loomed overhead, woven into the iron gate. "There are my two favorite guys. How was the sightseeing?"

Brandon couldn't hold back. "Fantastic! The cathedral was marvelous, and the views were out of this world. I stood on the very spot where Zwingli preached, back during the Swiss Reformation. Did you know that Charlemagne picked the location for the church?"

"I do now." She winked at her brother-in-law. "I see you took good care of our young charge."

"We both had fun." He glanced at his watch again. "I hate to run, but you know how Swiss bankers are about being punctual."

She waved her hands at him. "Run along. I'll get Brandon all to myself for a change." She touched his cheek and spoke with an exaggerated western accent. "Come on, pardner. We need to have ourselves a sit-down in this here place. We'll have ourselves some victuals and an old-fashioned powwow."

Brandon grinned and pulled away. "Just a minute." He ran after Rick and gave him a hug and quick kiss on his cheek. "I'll see you at the hotel this afternoon."

"I'll be there. Have a good time, you two." He waved goodbye and hustled off to the Oberdorf-Strasse to catch a cab while Brandon stood and watched.

Sandra called out to him from the gate, "Come on, dear. They have our table all ready for us."

He followed her inside and settled into his chair. "What's good to eat?" His arm throbbed, and he adjusted the sling.

Her somber eyes looked at his wounded limb. "It still hurts, doesn't it?"

"Some. It's a lot better, and my physical therapist says that I'm doing great. She thinks it'll be less than a year and then I'll be good as new."

"We haven't had much of a chance to talk, just the two of us, since New Year's Eve. I like chatting with you."

"I like being with you, too. You're fun to be around, Sandra, and you've always been good to me."

"I'm grateful to you for what you did. You were very brave."

"More like very stupid. I should have trusted Sam and just given him that key. He pretty much chewed me a new...er, chewed me out over it. But Rick's lawyer was so suspicious of everything, even Sam. I tried to call her, and there wasn't any answer, so I just went. I never thought anything could go wrong, just looking."

"And then that awful Daniels showed up. It was your quick thinking that saved the day."

"Can we not talk about it? I mean, I know you're grateful and all, but it's kind of an unpleasant memory."

"Sure." She examined the menu. "Shall I order for us?"

"Okay. Just be sure to include beer."

"So, tell me what interesting things you and Rick saw today, dear."

By the time their meal was over, Brandon ran out of tour guide data to enthuse over. "I'm sorry. I bet this is all boring to you. I know you've been here dozens of times before."

She smiled and touched his cheek. "You couldn't possibly bore me, Brandon. I understand what Rick sees in you." She opened her purse and pulled out an envelope.

"You've been through so much, and all you've gotten out of it is pain and suffering."

"That's not true! I got Rick out of it. And you, too. Friends forever, right?"

"I hope so." The envelope turned in her fingers. The music in the restaurant changed to a group singing an old Beatles hit in German. "Have you by any chance listened to the tape of Daniels' confession?"

He gave her a wary look. "Well, yeah. I studied Fran MacDonald's case file too, when I was in the hospital. Nothing much else to do, and I was kind of obsessed with it. My therapist told me it wasn't healthy, so I quit."

"I've read it, too. I guess we're both compulsive." A nervous smile fled across her features. "You know, he didn't exactly confess."

Brandon kept his face impassive. "I noticed that. It doesn't matter. The DA is certain he did it, and everyone I care about is free and clear." He looked her in the eye. "Everyone."

"You know, there was this one note in her file. It keeps rattling in my mind."

He shook his head. "Sandra, don't go there. I'm happy to leave things as they are."

She didn't look at him. Her fingers folded the envelope in half, and then unfolded it and smoothed the crease on the table in front of her. "I just can't get it out of my mind. She wrote, in big letters, 'follow the money,' right there in her case file. What do you suppose she meant by that?"

He sighed. "I think I don't want to know."

She glanced up, and then her eyes returned to the envelope. "Daniels couldn't have moved the money. He'd never even been to the bank. He couldn't have known the codes, or known about the security system. If you think about it, there's only one person who had means, motive, and opportunity, once you include the money in the equation."

Brandon shook his head. "Stop this. Please."

Her voice turned dreamy. "You know, I wondered why Victoria put her sex playroom in the same complex as our condo in Dubuque. She must have known that eventually Rick or I would see her there and confront her. It's like she wanted someone to know her secrets. Do you think it's true that people want to get caught when they do bad things?"

He stared at her without speaking. His breath came in short bursts.

At last her eyes met his. "Sometimes accidents happen. People do things, and they turn out bad, but that doesn't make them bad people. Don't you think that's true?"

"People are more than their deeds. Yes, I think that's true. But you don't need to do this, Sandra. I don't want to know more than I do."

She nodded. "But you do know. You're smart. I'm sure you've already figured it out. You're compassionate, too. I've never trusted in the kindness of strangers, but I trust you, Brandon." She paused and wiped a tear from her eye. "You know, the Catholics may have something. Confession seems to be good for the soul after all." Her eyes avoided his. "Before the Reformation, they used to sell indulgences too, as a kind of an insurance policy against God's grace." She thrust the envelope at him. "Here. This is for you."

He looked at it like it was a death warrant. "What is it?"

"It's a numbered account at the Schweizer Privatbank für Investitions und Sparungs, here in Zurich. Brian had an account there. So do I. And now, so do you. There's a lot of money in yours. Almost a third of the Montgomery Trust."

The tension that had been coiling in his gut released, and it wasn't a good feeling. Vomit burned his throat, and he gulped it back with beer. "I don't want it." He didn't touch the envelope.

"Please, take it for me, dear. We can't take back our sins, but we can do penance for them. This is part of mine." She shoved the envelope in his pocket and, for an instant, a light gleamed in her eyes.

He stared at her and let a gentle finger stroke her palm. "Why did you do it?" he whispered.

She lowered her gaze to the table. "It was an accident. We argued, I pushed her, and she fell down the stairs into the coal cellar. My own sister, in a pool of blood! I panicked, and then I saw the pesticide and it hit me. I could hide her body, just like they did on TV. The whole plan, moving the money to cover up her disappearance, using the pesticide, everything just cascaded into my head all at once. I wish it hadn't, but it did. It seemed like the perfect crime." A wild little laugh passed her lips. "In fact, it was the perfect crime. Only you were clever enough to figure it out."

"How about Steadman?"

She looked down, and her fingers traced little imaginary lines on the tablecloth. "I knew about the body bags, of course. I'd seen them the month before, when I confronted Victoria at her condo at the Lindermont Arms. When I went to get them, *he* was there. He laughed at me and taunted me about running off with Victoria. I slapped him, and then he hit me and threatened me with the gun. It went off, then he was dead, with his brains all over that bed." Tears flowed down her cheeks. "I left my car at our condo and used his rental to move the body. After that, I drove it on to Chicago and then dropped it off there." She sniffed and wiped her cheeks with her napkin. "It all just happened. I wish I could take it back, but I can't." She squeezed his hands and stared into his face. "I would never have let Rick take the blame. You have to believe me on that. I would have come forward."

"I believe you."

"Can you forgive me, Brandon?"

"Sandra, I think I understand you. I do love you, even yet. But forgiveness...that's not mine to give." His voice was firm, but his soul trembled. "You'll have to find that in your own heart, if you can."

She turned her head away. "I don't think I ever will." Silence endured for a moment, for an eternity. "What will you do now?"

"Now? I'm going back to the hotel to wait for Rick. We'll have dinner, make love, and then in the morning we'll take the train to Milan to see *The Last Supper*."

"Nothing else?"

A gentle smile played across his face. "What else is there in life besides love?"

About the Author

Max Griffin writes horror, science fiction, and suspense stories, often with a dark twist. Authors as diverse as John Updike, Dean Koontz, Richard Matheson, and Lawrence Block inspire and inform his literary style.

Max Griffin is the pen name of a mathematician and academic. Under his professional name, he is the author of a graduate textbook in real analysis and numerous research articles. When he is not writing fiction, he fills his days with teaching mathematics and statistics, research, and administrative work at a major comprehensive university in the southwest. He is the proud parent of a daughter who is a librarian. He is blessed to be in a long-term relationship with his life partner, Mr. Gene, who is an expert knitter.

The two humans in Max's household are the pets of an Abyssinian cat named Mr. Dinger, short for Erwin Schrodinger the Cat. Mr. Dinger graciously lets them live in his home in return for food and occasional petting. Oh, and there's that litter box thing they do for him too.

Max's website is at: http://maxgriffin.net

PURPLE SWORD PUBLICATIONS
Romance and Speculative Fiction
www.purplesword.com